Berr... K... book is bo... h a ri... hi... al d... t. Of all the 'dirt... Ame... ca in the 1960's and 1970s, the... abou... outside the country and only n... debated within the country. Kucinsk... ...combative editor during the long period of successive military dictatorships (which took him into exile to work for the *Guardian* and the BBC), and here he uses the techniques of literary fiction to tell the true story of a father searching for his 'disappeared' daughter in those dark times. The narrator, himself a refugee from the authoritarian Poland of the 1930s, with a family lost subsequently in the Holocaust, reflects in a series of beautifully observed sketches on both the bravery and foolhardiness of resistance, as well as on the moral opacity of people and institutions that should have known better how to react. Always gripping, the story unfolds in a series of snapshots that give a real feeling for the period, emphasising both the particularity of Brazil's experience and its place in the wider scheme of things in the darkest moments of the twentieth century.

Richard Gott, former literary editor of the Guardian

This important and powerful novel evokes universal themes and characters, from the kidnapper who cannot harm a dog to the torturer's mistress and – unforgettably – the father who cannot stop searching for his disappeared daughter. Lyrically translated from the Portuguese, it should be required reading for those who see Brazil simply as an economic success story, without understanding the trauma of its recent history. Highly recommended.

Lindsey Hilsum, International Editor, Channel 4 News

A masterpiece, magisterial, more than this, unique.

Alípio Freire, poet, editor and former political prisoner

This is a substantial literary work, not only because it registers and bears witness to history, but also because it throws light on State Terrorism as a form of political and social control that exterminates those who oppose it.

Hamilton Pereira (Pedro Tierra), poet, former political prisoner, and currently Culture Secretary in the Federal District Government in Brazil

Few tales have left such an impression on me, both for the tragic force of the narrative and for the feeling of revolt that it arouses in the reader. K manages to transform the real story lived by the father into a metaphor and an indictment of the inhumanity and cruelty of a regime of oppression.

J. Guinsburg, Brazilian translator and writer

I couldn't stop reading from the first page to the last. I was impressed with the vigour of the narrative, the sensitivity with which the theme was treated and the theme itself.

Gilberto Maringoni, Brazilian journalist and cartoonist

Even the system, which in Kafka is impersonal and alienating, is revealed in this work in its hierarchical, violent and indifferent variants, whether perverse or sophisticated ... The protagonist is portrayed with magisterial skill with his thoughts and his pain ... The tales demonstrate the evil, indifference, complicity, opportunism and moral decadence of a society under military dictatorship.

Avraham Milgram, historian, Museum of the Holocaust, Jerusalem

Far from suggesting coldness or emotional distance, the sparseness of the narrative style puts the reader in a permanent state of alert confronted with the minefield of the text, waiting for the bomb of pain that is about to explode ... In the preface to *The Great Journey*, the Spanish writer Jorge Semprún says he needed sixteen years to acquire sufficient distance to write about his time in a concentration camp. Kucinski needed more time than this because he went further than the introspection needed to reconstitute the past in the first person. He took the perspective of his father, ever more desperate and worn down, ever more obstinate ...

Maria Rita Kehl, writer, poet and psycho-analyst

Of all the books I've read about this period, this is the one I found most moving.

Maria Victória Benevides, sociologist, historian, writer, member of the Justice and Peace Commission in São Paulo

It's a wonderful book. It moved the ground under my feet and this ground has been stationary for a long while. The very unusual structure of the narrative reinforces its power. As the long and painful rosary of memory is played out, K takes off and gains power and space.

Eric Nepomuceno, writer, translator, journalist

What brings together the narrative, apart from the factual continuity of the father seeking his daughter and son-in-law in the entrails of the dictatorship, is the construction of contemporary consciousness, of the writer confronted with his own memory.

Flávio Aguiar, lecturer in literature, writer, journalist

K is an extraordinary book. Very well written, a profound and piercing reflection on loss and resistance to dictatorship.

Ottoni Fernandes Junior, journalist, writer, publisher and former political prisoner

A remarkable book! One of the best accounts, perhaps the very best, written on the theme of the disappeared.

Vladimir Sachetta, writer, historian, journalist

Everything in this book is invented but almost everything
happened.

K

Bernardo Kucinski

translated by Sue Branford

with drawings by
Enio Squeff

Latin America Bureau

K was first published in English in 2013 by Latin America Bureau
www.lab.org.uk

K was written in Portuguese and first published in Brazil
in 2011 (revised edition 2012) by
Editora Expressão Popular
Rua Abolição 201, Bela Vista
CEP 01319-010 São Paulo-SP, Brazil
www.expressaopopular.com.br

A catalogue record for this book is available from the British Library

Designed and typeset by Ralph Smith
Cover adapted from a design by ZAP Design
Printed and bound in the EU by
MPG Printgroup, Bodmin

ISBN 978-1-899365-77-7

This work is published with the support of the
Brazilian Ministry of Culture / National Library Foundation

MINISTÉRIO DA CULTURA
Fundação BIBLIOTECA NACIONAL

To her friends who lost her
suddenly
a world of intimacy fell apart

Contents

Foreword

During the last quarter of the twentieth century, as South America became a Cold War battlefield, a new phrase entered the lexicon of political terror: 'the disappeared'.

Thousands of men and women, and several hundred children, were seized in the street, abducted from their homes or kidnapped from their workplaces, never to be seen again. Some were members of armed guerrilla groups fighting the military juntas that had taken power by overthrowing elected presidents. Most were non-violent members of trade unions, student organisations, political parties or progressive churches, who believed in democracy and a fairer society. In some cases the crime was simply to be the mother, brother or child of a disappeared dissident, and to want to know what had happened to them.

I was a member of an ecumenical group called the Committee for the Defence of Human Rights in the Southern Cone, known as CLAMOR. It was set up in 1978 under the auspices of the Archbishop of São Paulo, Cardinal Paulo Evaristo Arns, to help political exiles and denounce the repression taking place in the region. It was very similar to the group described in the second chapter – 'The vortex' – and referred to elsewhere in *K*.

Human rights groups in Argentina, Chile and other countries began to publish appeals to the authorities for information, accompanied by ever longer lists of those who had disappeared. As we received list after list, we decided that it was important to show that each of the thousands of names referred to an individual – a husband, a daughter, a son. We ended up with a list of names of well over seven thousand people.

In *K*, Bernardo Kucinski goes further by turning the anguish of the families of the disappeared into a powerful work of literature. By imagining in detail the day-to-day struggle of one man to find his disappeared daughter, the frustrations and incomprehensions, the occasional short-lived glimmers of hope, he is also telling the story of thousands of others who, against all odds, fear, intimidation, lies and deceit, never gave up the search for their loved ones.

He shows how the burden of proof was shifted by the authorities to the families, who had to prove over and over again that the disappeared person actually existed. The burden of guilt also became theirs, the endless 'ifs' – if I had spoken to so and so, if I had tried this, gone there, done that, maybe I would have found him or her.

Just as remarkably, Bernardo Kucinski also gets into the minds of the armed-struggle protagonists. He recreates the drama of those so deeply involved in the clandestine struggle that dying for the cause became a matter of loyalty rather than a rational choice. He depicts the terror of a young, uneducated woman who ends up working in a house where torturers inflict unimaginable horrors on the disappeared. He tells the extraordinary – and true – story of a woman who seduced the most powerful man of the political-repression apparatus to save her brother and then, against her will, fell head over heels in love with this monstrous man, with disastrous results.

All twenty-eight chapters of this book, written in sparse, contained language, may be read separately. Together they add up to an extraordinary account of what political repression means for those involved in it, a compelling tale that is hard to put down. It presents one of the best pictures I know of the ways the dictatorships in South America distorted and undermined so many aspects of life, not only for the victims and their families, but for everyone who lived through it. The stories resonate beyond Brazil to every country that has experienced political repression.

The disappearances in Argentina, Chile, Brazil, and to a lesser extent Uruguay, Paraguay, Bolivia, and other Latin American countries, were an essential part of the Cold War: an instrument of the reign of terror installed in these countries under the national security doctrine coordinated by the USA to keep its 'backyard' – Central and South America – free of communism, even if it meant keeping it free of democracy.

Under national security law the armed forces of each country not only fought their own people, called the 'internal enemy', they collaborated intensely with each other. They crossed national borders with impunity to hunt down dissidents. Operation Condor was the name given to the collaboration among the intelligence services. Their targets included not just anonymous exiles, but former presidents, ministers and congress members who might lead opposition to the generals. They were murdered in cold blood wherever they were: the assassination of Salvador Allende's former minister, Orlando Letelier, took place in the centre of Washington DC.

Brazil, which in 1964 was the first country in the region to suffer a US-supported right-wing coup, became an exporter of torture techniques, passing on lessons learned from the USA and post-colonial France.

The human toll of the ideological war waged in South America was huge: in Argentina alone up to thirty thousand people disappeared. In Uruguay, which had the highest proportion of political prisoners in the world, a third of the population went into exile. In Brazil at least fifty thousand people were arbitrarily arrested and twenty thousand were tortured.

By the late 1970s, as the other countries sank deeper into the horrors of unbridled terror, the military government in Brazil had wiped out the armed opposition, and the country was submerged in economic problems, ballooning inflation and foreign debt. It was time to begin the gradual process of extricating the military from the mess they had created. In 1979 an amnesty law was passed that let off the hook those who had murdered and tortured in the name of the Free World. Amnesty became amnesia.

Within a few years of restoring civilian government, other countries emerging from dictatorships in the 1980s or 1990s set up commissions to investigate the disappearances and deaths and to punish the guilty. Brazil, by contrast, has taken twenty-seven years to establish a Truth Commission to investigate the crimes of the military dictatorship. Even now the Commission can only investigate and cannot bring anyone to trial, however damning the evidence against them. Torturers and murderers continue to cower behind the amnesty law, safe from prosecution.

But for how long? Some public prosecutors have begun to explore loopholes in the law. By revealing the full extent of what happened, Brazil's Truth Commission may provide the incentive for repealing the 1979 amnesty law. The Commission will look at the facts. Bernardo's book reminds us of what those facts meant to the families left behind.

Jan Rocha

Acknowledgements

I would like to thank all those who helped me with criticisms and suggestions: Avraham Milgram, Bernardo Zeltzer, Carlos Knapp, Flamarion Maués, Flávio Aguiar, Venício Lima and Zilda Junqueira; Dina Lida Kinoshita for her help in the use of Yiddish and for the street map of Warsaw; Cláudio Ceri for help with the language in the Left in the Lurch section; and my wife, Mutsuko, for everything.

Latin America Bureau would like to thank Nick Caistor, Mike Gatehouse, Francis McDonagh, Linda Rabben, Ralph Smith and David Treece for their help with the translation and editing of this book.

K

What I'm telling you about, mister, is the things I know and you don't; but chiefly I want to tell you about the things I don't know if I know, and that maybe you do.

Guimarães Rosa, *Grande Sertão: Veredas*

It's not the pain of no longer believing
That overwhelms me, or of not knowing,
Only (and more) utterly the awfulness
Of having seen the mystery face to face,
Of having seen and understood it in all
The boundlessness of its mystery

Fernando Pessoa, 'O mistério do mundo'

I set this story alight, and snuff myself out. At the end of these writings, I shall be a voiceless shadow once more.

Mia Couto, *Terra Sonâmbula*

Letters to someone who doesn't exist

Every so often, the postman delivers a letter to her at my old address. From a bank, offering an enticing new product or financial service. The most recent one introduced a new credit card, valid on every continent, ideal for making hotel and airline reservations. Something she might well have found useful, if her life hadn't been interrupted. All you have to do is sign the form and return it in the enclosed pre-paid envelope, said the last letter.

It always moves me to see her name on the envelope. And I ask myself: how is it possible they keep on sending letters to someone who hasn't existed for over three decades? I know it's not in bad faith. Neither the post office nor the bank knows that she no longer exists: their logos, far from being hidden, are proudly – garishly – displayed. With its marble pillars that give a false impression of solidity, the bank is an expression of the system: it deals with computer lists, not with faces and people.

The woman these proposals are sent to will never accept them, even though there is no annual charge for the credit card, even though she can accumulate air miles and use VIP waiting rooms at airports. All this she could have had but won't, all this offered to her now that she doesn't exist, all this that scarcely existed when she existed. An inventory of losses from the loss of a life.

It is as if the letters had the hidden intention of not allowing her memory to rest in our memory; it's as if the system, as well as denying us her body so that we cannot heal through mourning, has turned the postman into a Dybbuk,[1] a tormented soul constantly pointing out what we did wrong and what we failed to do. It is as if, as well as causing an unnecessary death, the system wants now to ruin necessary life, life that goes on and generates demands from children and grandchildren.

Why do the letters go to my old address? For a long while I thought that at one of those uncertain moments in the midst of flight and pretence, of escaping round corners, she'd given the bank my address so that she wouldn't have to give other genuine but forbidden ones. I used to try to imagine at what stage in the evolving tragedy this had happened, what address she'd had at the time or, more accurately, what addresses she'd had, because I discovered that she'd had many addresses, believing that was how she could outwit destiny.

In fact, they weren't homes, places to bring up children and entertain friends. They were anti-homes, catacombs she could lie low in for months, like the early Christians in Rome, or just for weeks or days, until someone was captured, and then the ordeal would begin again with a frantic search for a new hiding place.

That must have been why she didn't give the address of the catacomb she was using at the time, but that of the house where my wife, my sons and I lived for thirty-three years; and where my older son and my grandson now live, and where I still have my office and my wife has her vegetable garden and her art studio and my grandson has his two dogs and his toys.

It was only then I realised that if I had sold this house, as I had often thought of doing, I would have lost the reference points of half my life. It was only then that I understood what my older son had meant when he said no, this house is never to be sold. For him, this house holds all his memories.

---

1   In Jewish mythology a Dybbuk is an unsatisfied soul who clings to a person, generally to torment him or her. The word derives from the Hebrew word Devek, which means glue.

Then it occurred to me that I'd got it wrong. She never knew this house. I worked it out and discovered that it was six years after she'd disappeared that we bought this run-down house, from elderly Portuguese immigrants. No, she never knew our house. She never knew the steep steps up through the front garden. She never knew my sons. She was never able to be my children's aunt. This is one of the things I most regret of everything that happened.

If she didn't have this address, who gave it to the system? A mystery. How did her name get attached to my address in the shadowy world of the Internet, where nothing is deleted? The most likely explanation is that I myself made the link. Was it when I requested an official 'missing person' declaration? Was it when I asked the lawyer to deal with the assets she left? Was it when I asked the university to revoke its shameful act of sacking her for abandoning her job? I will never know when it happened. All I know is that letters addressed to someone who doesn't exist will keep on arriving.

The postman will never know that this person doesn't exist, that she was kidnapped, tortured and murdered by the military dictatorship. Just as, before him, the man in the sorting office and everyone else working in the post office will never know. The name on the envelope, sealed and stamped as if to give it the seal of authenticity, is evidence not of a computer defect, but of Alzheimer's on a national scale. Yes, the continued presence of her name among the living is, paradoxically, the result of the way the nation has collectively forgotten its dead.

São Paulo, 31 December 2010

3

The vortex

The tragedy was already unstoppable when for the first time that Sunday morning K felt the anguish that would soon engulf him. His daughter hadn't phoned for ten days. Later, he would blame the lack of routines in his family, routines that become more necessary in difficult times – a daily phone call, Sunday lunches. His daughter didn't get on with his second wife.

And how had he, such a seasoned political observer, failed to notice the recent turmoil in the country? Would it have been different if, instead of having Yiddish writers as friends, connoisseurs of a dead language that only a few old people still spoke, he'd paid more attention to what was going on? How could he tell? Was Yiddish important?[1] Not at all. A corpse whose death they lamented in weekly meetings, instead of looking after the living.

Ever since he'd brought her back little presents from the Sunday market, he'd associated Sundays with his daughter. Suddenly, he recalled rumours he'd heard the day before in Bom Retiro:[2] it seemed that two Jewish medical students,

1 Yiddish, the language of Jews in Eastern Europe, reached its high point at the beginning of the twentieth century, when its literature became more established; it declined rapidly because of the Holocaust and because the Israeli state adopted Hebrew as its official language.
2 A Jewish quarter of São Paulo.

one of them apparently from a rich family, had disappeared. Something to do with politics and the dictatorship, people said, nothing to do with anti-Semitism. Others, non-Jews, had disappeared as well, so the Jewish Federation had decided not to do anything. This was what the people had said. But he wasn't sure it was true because no one seemed to know the students' names.

It was the rumour that had upset him, not the fact that it was a Sunday. He spent the day dialling the number his daughter had given him for emergencies but the phone rang and rang. No reply, not even at one o'clock in the morning when she ought to have been back, even if she'd been to the cinema, something she enjoyed so much. He decided to look for her at the university the next day.

That night he dreamed of the time when the Cossacks had invaded his father's cobbler's shop to make him repair their boots. He'd only been a child at the time. He woke up with a shudder. The Cossacks, he remembered, had arrived precisely on Tisha B'Av,[3] the Jewish day of mourning for all the tragedies that have befallen the Jewish people, the day of the destruction of the First Temple and the Second Temple, the day of the expulsion from Spain.

Without knowing what there was to be alarmed about, but alarmed none the less, he got up without waking his wife, took his Austin out of the garage and drove to the university campus beyond the jungle of skyscrapers. He drove slowly, taking his time to cross the centre, as if he wanted the journey to go on for ever; his emotions lurched from confidence one moment that he would find her there, working normally, to despair the next moment that the opposite would be the case. Finally he reached the chemistry block, which he'd visited only once before, years earlier, when his daughter had defended her

3   Literally, it means the ninth day in the month of Av, which is considered cursed in the Jewish calendar.

doctoral thesis before a group of stern-faced lecturers, some of them educated in Germany.

She's not in today, her colleagues said. They glanced hesitantly at one another. Then, as if afraid the walls might hear what they were saying, they took K into the garden. There they told him she hadn't been in for eleven days. Yes, precisely eleven days, including the weekends. She, who never let her students down, never missed a lecture. They whispered, speaking in half-sentences, as if behind each word lurked another thousand words they couldn't utter.

Agitated, dissatisfied with what he'd been told, K insisted on speaking to the head of the department – surely he'd know more? If she'd had an accident and been hospitalised, surely the university would have been informed? But her friends got alarmed. Don't do that. Not yet. To be more persuasive, they changed their tone: she could have gone away, they said, gone off for a few days as a precaution. Strangers had been asking after her. There were some strange people on the campus. They were writing down number plates. They were operating from the chancellor's office. Who were they? Nobody could tell him.

Finally convinced not to speak to the authorities, K, distraught, drove from the campus to a house in Padre Chico Street, an address his daughter had given him some time ago, telling him he should go there only if something very serious happened and he couldn't get her on the phone. Why hadn't he questioned her properly about this business of only going there if something serious happened? Why had he accepted it when she told him to phone only if it was urgent? How stupid he'd been. What had he been thinking of? Oh God!

The address was a terraced house, which gave directly on to the street, squeezed among a dozen similar houses. Leaflets and dusty newspapers on the doorstep suggested the house had been empty for a long while. Nobody answered when he rang the doorbell insistently.

The enormity of his predicament hit him. What could he do? His two sons were far away, abroad. His second wife, useless. His daughter's university friends, panicking. The old man felt crushed by it all. His body felt weak, empty, as if it were about to collapse. His mind was numb. Suddenly, nothing else was important. A single fact dominated, cancelling out everything that wasn't part of it. All that mattered was the concrete fact that his beloved daughter had been missing for eleven days, perhaps longer. He felt completely alone.

He mentally made a list of possible explanations. Perhaps she'd had an accident or a serious illness she didn't want anyone to know about. But the one explanation that kept coming back was the most serious – that she'd been arrested by the secret services. The State is faceless and impassive, impervious and perverse. Its only weak point is corruption. But sometimes even access this way becomes impossible, on orders from above. And then the State becomes doubly malignant – cruel and unapproachable. He knew this very well from his own experience.

K recalled his recent contacts with his daughter, her nervousness, her evasive answers, her habit of arriving in a hurry and leaving in a hurry, her insistence he should only go to her house in an emergency and not pass her address on to anyone. With dismay he realised just how far he had been deceiving himself. Tricked by his own daughter, who was perhaps involved in extremely dangerous activities without him realising it, distracted as he was by his devotion to Yiddish, by the easy seduction of literary circles.

Ah, and the mistake of marrying that German Jewess only because she knew how to cook potatoes. He cursed his friends who'd persuaded him to marry again. He cursed them all. He, who never blasphemed, who tolerantly accepted people as they were, found himself out of control, raving. With a dull foreboding that his worst fears would be realised.

A writer friend, who was also a lawyer, advised him on the phone to register her disappearance with the Department for Missing Persons; it wouldn't help, he added, but it was something a father had to do. He gave him the address, in Brigadeiro Tobías Avenue, the police headquarters. K asked him if he'd heard that two Jewish medical students had disappeared. Yes. It was true. One of the families had been to see him. What was he going to do? Nothing. The courts had been forbidden to accept petitions for habeas corpus in political cases. There's nothing a lawyer can do, he said. Nothing. That's how it is.

At the police station they weren't very interested. Most missing people were teenagers running away from alcoholic parents or stepfathers who beat them. K explained that his daughter was a university lecturer, with a doctorate, that she was independent and lived by herself. She had her own car. Perhaps it was something political?

He didn't want to go into details with the police official, he only hinted. So he didn't give the Padre Chico Street address, gave his own as if it were hers and the shop address as if it were his. Without noticing it, K was reactivating the long-dormant habits of his conspiratorial youth in Poland. The police official became uneasy. He wasn't allowed to get involved in political cases. But, feeling sorry for the old man, he registered the case, telling him to wait and not to mention politics.

Look for her? No, the police had too much to do. A grown-up university lecturer, just over 30 years old. He should wait, a circular with her photograph would go out to all stations. If he hadn't heard anything after five days, he should go to the morgue, which received unidentified bodies from road accidents and other disasters. He looked embarrassed as he said this.

And so the old man began his odyssey, more anguished and more exhausted with each passing day. On the twentieth day, after yet another vain trip to the campus and to Padre Chico Street, he went back to his friends in the literary circle, the ones he'd sworn about when he lost his temper. Perhaps one of them would know someone who knew someone in the police, the army, the secret services, anywhere in that system that swallowed people up, leaving no trace. But, except for the lawyer, they were old, poor people who didn't know anyone important. The lawyer mentioned vaguely a Jewish community leader in Rio de Janeiro who had access to the generals. He would try and find out more.

K began to count the days his daughter had been missing, another habit that came from his youth. And not a day passed without him trying to do something for his daughter. In fact, he didn't do anything else. He had to take pills at night to sleep. On the twenty-fifth day of his daughter's disappearance, he plucked up the courage to go to the morgue.

Without mentioning politics, he told them that his daughter had disappeared. He showed them a photo of her on her graduation day, looking distinguished. And then another, at a later time, when she looked thin and unhappy. No, the employees didn't recognise her among the few recent female corpses, all black or of mixed race. Almost all of them beggars. To tell the truth, it must be over a year since they'd had the corpse of an unidentified white woman. K left the morgue relieved; he could still hope to find her alive. But the photographs of the beggars and nameless people had depressed him. He'd never seen such ravaged faces, such scared eyes, even during the war in Poland.

It was then that he began to talk obsessively to customers who came into his shop to make their monthly payments, to neighbours and even to strangers. He told all of them his daughter's story. And, he stressed, her Beetle car had disappeared too. Most listened to the end in silence, gave him a pat on the back, and said: I'm really sorry. Some, a few, interrupted him at the beginning, claiming to have a doctor's appointment or inventing another pretext – as if just to hear him out would put them in danger.

On the thirtieth day, K read an article in the *Estado de S. Paulo* newspaper that referred obliquely to political disappearances. The archbishop was to hold a meeting with 'the families of disappeared political activists'. It was written just like that: 'the families of disappeared political activists'.

K had never been in a Catholic church before, so alien had its silent gloom and the images of saints appeared to him when he'd glanced through the door. He felt an atavistic revulsion towards Catholicism, along with his scorn for religious rites of all kinds, including those practised by his own people. To be more accurate, it wasn't the people and their beliefs he disliked, it was the clergy, whether they were priests, rabbis or bishops; he considered them all hypocrites. But none of this mattered on that afternoon. An important authority, an archbishop, was going to talk about the strange disappearances.

As he went into the main room in the archdiocesan offices, K realised how much the disappearance of his daughter had already changed him. He was looking with sympathy at the baroque image of the Virgin Mary in the centre of the room and at the other saints he didn't know in the corners. When he arrived, the meeting had already begun. There were at least sixty people sitting on the numerous chairs laid out around the room. Seated in a half-moon in front of the public, four serious men who looked like lawyers were coordinating the meeting; a nun was taking notes in a large book.

A very old woman, perhaps over 90, slight, frail, with white hair and glasses on the end of her nose, was speaking; on his way back into the country from exile, her husband had arrived in Uruguaiana, on the frontier with Uruguay, where he'd gone to a pre-arranged meeting on the Brazilian side of the frontier; and then he'd disappeared completely, without a trace, as if he'd vanished into thin air or the angels had carried him off to heaven. One of his sons had tried to track him down and been to all the hospitals, police stations, bus stations in Uruguaiana, and found nothing, nothing at all. Her son, at her side, corroborated her account.

Then another woman, in her 50s, spoke; she introduced herself as the wife of a former federal deputy. Two policemen had come to their house, asked her husband to go with them to the police station to answer a few questions. He'd gone with them unconcerned because, although he'd been expelled from Congress by the military, he led a normal life and ran a legal practice. Since then, eight months ago, he hadn't been seen. The police said they had only held him there for a quarter of an hour and then let him go. What could have happened? How could he have disappeared so completely? This elegantly dressed woman was accompanied by her four children.

More stories of disappearances – everyone wanted to speak. And to listen. They wanted to understand what was happening. Perhaps out of all these cases an explanation would emerge, a rationale and above all a solution, a way of ending the nightmare. A young woman, no more than 20 years old, asked to speak in the name of a group seated around her, 'the families of the disappeared from Araguaia', she said. This was the first time K heard anyone speak about Araguaia, how a large group of young men and some young women had been captured by the armed forces in the middle of the Amazon forest and immediately executed.[4]

This group had come to the meeting for a strange reason.

---

4 Araguaia is a region around the river of the same name in the Brazilian Amazon. A guerrilla group was set up here in the early 1970s to fight the military dictatorship, but their activities were discovered at an early stage, and all but one of their members were captured and killed, and their bodies disposed of in the forest.

The army claimed they were inventing the whole story, even though one of the prisoners, just one, had escaped, having witnessed it all. But the families knew that their loved ones, more than fifty of them they said, were dead and they wanted to bury them. They even knew more or less where in the region they'd been killed, but the military kept on insisting that there were no bodies to hand over.

A young man had met his wife for lunch in the Conjunto Nacional, a building in the centre of the city, and neither of them had been seen since. As she spoke, the man's mother displayed photos of her son, her daughter-in-law and her little grandson. Then a man got up, saying he'd come specially from Goiânia for the meeting. His two sons, one 20 and the other only 16, had both disappeared. This man stuttered, he seemed dazed. He was the first to use the expression: "they were disappeared." He also held up photos of his sons. After him, K found the courage to tell his story.

Night fell and still the reports went on. The scenarios varied, the details, the circumstances, but all the twenty-two cases recorded at that meeting shared one fearful characteristic: the people had disappeared without trace. It was the same with the youngsters in Araguaia, although the families knew that they were dead. The nun recorded the cases one by one. She also collected the photos the families had brought.

K listened to everything, horrified. Even the Nazis, who'd reduced their victims to ashes, had registered the dead. Each one had had a number, tattooed on his or her arm. They'd noted each death in a book. It's true there had been massacres in the first days after an invasion and at the end too. They'd made all the Jews in a village line up along a ditch, shot them, thrown lime over them and then earth. But even then the goyim[5] in each place had known where to find the ditch where their Jews had been buried, how many they were and who they were. There hadn't been this agony of uncertainty. These had been mass executions, not people vanishing into thin air.

5 Yiddish for non-Jewish people; the singular is goy.

The trap

Outside, life goes on as ever: women go shopping, labourers work, children play, beggars beg, lovers make love. Inside, in the small one-bedroom flat, panic has taken hold of the couple. Their hands shake. You can hear the fear in their voices. They can't look each other in the eye. They sweat, exuding terror. There's no other explanation for what happened at the meeting: they've been betrayed. There's an informer among them, a turncoat or an infiltrator, someone very close to them, someone from the small group of survivors.

It happened only two hours ago. The instructions they had received were clear and unequivocal: you must assume the worst, you must assume that the comrade they seized will break under torture and talk. You haven't the time or the peace of mind to work out precisely what he knew or didn't know. According to the instructions, you must assume he knew everything.

Fortunately, he'd been doubly careful. Or had he already felt in his bones that something was wrong? He'd arrived an hour early, hiding himself away, where he could see the square without being seen. And he'd spotted disguised agents arriving one by one, placing themselves around, in the centre, on the sides. At least ten of them.

So he'd seen when the contact arrived, dejected, stumbling, agitated, and had sat down on the bench as arranged and begun to wait the stipulated five minutes, never more than five minutes, according to their security instructions.

He himself didn't wait five minutes. He'd seen enough. A trap. The contact himself was the bait, it seemed. But someone else could also have betrayed him. The regional command knew about the meeting as well.

What should they do? Months before, when their leader had been caught, the solution had been obvious. They should have simply accepted defeat and suspended the struggle. Pulled back, saving themselves for other battles in the future. That morning, it wasn't so easy, although the way out was along the same lines, the only possible action, and less complicated than it seemed. Recognise defeat. Admit that it's finished. We lost. The struggle is over. Burn papers, cancel plans, destroy evidence, no more meetings, ignore the phone, have nothing to do with contacts. But it would be decades before the few survivors would admit, with hindsight, that the only solution at the time had been to accept defeat.

At that moment, isolated and alone in the small flat, the couple don't understand this, they don't think like this. They're still assessing the degree of danger. The fallen comrade knows their code names, he can hand over fragments of information that lead to names, locations, dates. They try to remember if they followed the security instructions in their phone call with him. Yes, they arranged to meet on the day after the real one and for an hour after the real hour. Always a day later and an hour later, they'd been told.

They need to hurry. The person who set up the meeting might also be a traitor. So there might be two different sources of danger. At any moment one of them could speak. If they were quick, they might be able to preserve the normal half of their lives, that is, life itself.

The couple had proper identity cards, stable jobs, fa
friends, parents and siblings. The non-clandestine half o
lives was intact. They just needed to give up the secret half,
to delete it – as one would say today, using this expressive
neologism – not because they were cowards but because they
were clever. To save themselves, to survive in defeat would be
a victory, a real victory. Even if it wasn't possible to delete, they
could always seek refuge in a hideout somewhere, in someone's
holiday home, in an embassy, in the cathedral. But first they
had to admit defeat. The key to the solution was accepting
defeat, accepting that the struggle was over.

But both carry on. They don't behave lucidly. They're
not governed by the logic of political struggle but by other
logics, perhaps of guilt, solidarity, despair. They put in a small
briefcase two crudely forged passports, plans for armed action
that'll never be carried out because the war is already lost, a
revolver and some cartridges, perhaps ones that won't even
fit, and the pre-nuptial agreement they'd drawn up to try to
protect the other if one were taken.

They stuff into a larger canvas bag what they see as the
most important of the documents they've laboriously gathered
– a list of 232 torturers, who will never be punished, even
decades after their names have been widely publicised, even
decades after the dictatorship has ended; the political prisoners'
manifestoes; the dossier on torture; the report promised to
Amnesty International. And also the file with press cuttings
about the habits and routines of the businessmen who financed
the torture centres. They don't know it, but, except for the
man who's already been assassinated for his crimes, all the
others will have roads named in their honour and will die in
their beds from natural causes, surrounded by their children,
grandchildren and friends.

And what can they do with the two duplicators they
expropriated from an academic institute? They will have to

leave them behind. Just like the books, the dozens of books on history, Marxist theory and economics, Marighella's manual on urban guerrilla warfare, Debray's book, Marta Harnecker's texts, and the strange, unsettling books by Nietzsche, defending the invincible force of individual will against the dominant morality.

Outside, life goes on as ever: the economy grows, women shop, children play, beggars beg, lovers kiss. The couple could try to survive to recommence the struggle later, in other conditions, on other terms. But no. The last task they each do is insert a small cyanide capsule in a gap between their teeth. A long time ago they swore never to be captured alive, so that they wouldn't betray their comrades under torture. There is nothing about cyanide capsules in the instructions.

The informers

Alongside the visible world, which reassures us with its 'good morning's, its 'good afternoon's and its 'how are you?'s, there is another world, a hidden world of obscenities and depravities. It is in this world that informers flourish. If it hadn't been for the kidnapping of his daughter, K would never have discovered this other world so close to his own. But they'd always been there, lurking, the police informers. To start with, courteous Caio, pallid and effeminate, who for years had been designing shop windows, moving adroitly among the mannequins, with the pins of his official trade held between his tightened lips.

As soon as he arrived to redecorate the windows for winter, K spoke to him. 'My daughter's been missing for five weeks', he says. 'Five weeks', he repeats, ignoring the 'how are you?'. He pulls him into his cubby-hole at the back of the shop. There, forced to sit down, the decorator listens to the old man's dramatic monologue with its anguished gestures. When it ends, Caio says in a sorrowful voice that he's very sorry. And then suggests they get on with the windows.

But, once the work is over, the decorator takes him for a coffee in the *padaria*[1] on the corner. As they stand at the

1   In Brazil, as in Portugal, a *padaria* – 'bakery' – provides a range of other services supplied in most other countries by mini-markets and coffee shops.

counter, he confides that he has friends in the police. He says in a self-important way that through his work he gets to know Syrians in Brás, Jews in Bom Retiro, Germans in Brooklin. The government wants to know what these foreigners are up to, he says, and he keeps an eye on everything. He promises to help. He's going to try to find out if K's daughter was arrested and, if she was, where they've taken her.

It's quite a shock, Caio a police informer. Perturbed, K hurriedly writes the name and age of his daughter on a paper napkin. A lecturer in chemistry in the University of São Paulo, he adds.

On the following day Amadeu, the Portuguese owner of the *padaria*, turns up in his shop. He asks to see a shirt. The two – the Jew and the Portuguese man – have known each other for twenty years. While he pretends to examine the shirt, Amadeu talks about his *padaria*, how painful it is to stand for hours on end on the raised slat inside the booth where he takes payments. But it's only when he's standing there, he says, that he can see the whole of the *padaria*. He'd noticed Caio whispering to him as they stood at the counter and he'd guessed they were talking about the disappearance of his daughter, which was common knowledge in the street.

A good *padaria*, continues Amadeu, is not just a place for buying bread but a club, a meeting place, just like pharmacies in rural areas. Do you know how many conversations take place at my counter? More than two thousand people come into my *padaria* each day and more than three thousand on Saturdays and Sundays. *Padarias* are very useful to the police, he explains. He's going to try and find out if K's daughter is in prison. He asks for details about her and returns to the *padaria*, without buying the shirt.

If Caio and Amadeu are informers, then there must be spies everywhere, concludes K, in astonishment. It's true that when he arrived in Brazil in 1935, fleeing the Polish police, his fellow countrymen had warned him about Getúlio's[2] spies, 'zei zainem umetum', they're everywhere, they had cautioned in Yiddish. But that was under fascism. And, lo and behold, here are the spies again, everywhere.

Or perhaps they never went away? He begins to think so. The government may not always use the information, but the informers never stopped informing. When the government was repressive, like Getúlio's, it had used it. Hadn't Getúlio discovered where Olga[3] and many others were hiding through informers? What had been done to Olga was abominable. When the government was more tolerant it used the informers less.

With these thoughts running through his head, K starts to think he should contact the owner of the chemist's in Bom Retiro, a young man with such a vocation for spying that, when he was still only 20 years old, he was the leading informer about Jews in São Paulo. K had known his deceased father, who'd studied in Vilnius and enjoyed Yiddish literature. He died deeply ashamed of having a nark for a son, though the young man was tolerated by the community because he'd helped a large number of Jewish refugees who'd fled the Nazis without their papers in order and hadn't charged much. Fellow countrymen who got into scrapes also turned to him to negotiate an honourable way out with the police. K asks himself why he hadn't gone to him as soon as he'd found out about the inexplicable disappearance of his daughter.

It's then that Caio, the window dresser, phones. Yes, his daughter has been arrested. That's all I could find out. Tomorrow I'll know more. Don't phone, I'll phone you. The

2 Getúlio Dornelles Vargas came to power in Brazil in 1930 at the head of a military rebellion led by young officers, and in 1937 he set up a pro-fascist dictatorship that lasted until 1945. He was elected to power as President in 1950 and committed suicide in 1954.
3 Olga Benário Prestes was a German communist activist of Jewish origin and the wife of the Brazilian communist leader Luis Carlos Prestes. At the request of the Nazis she was extradited to Germany, and in 1942, at the age of 34, she was put to death in the Bernburg extermination camp.

same afternoon, a lad working in the *padaria* comes to tell K that his order is ready. K understands. He goes to the *padaria* and, waiting for a quiet moment without a queue of customers at the booth, he goes up and asks in a loud voice how much he owes for the order. Amadeu whispers: she's been arrested, I only know that. I'll know more in a few days. K is jubilant: she's alive; they weren't going to say she'd been arrested if she was dead. Both of them had said the same thing. He feels hugely relieved, more than words can say. Now all he has to do is wait until they discover where she is.

But two days later Amadeu summons him and whispers that there's been a mistake, she was never arrested, never, he repeats emphatically. Amadeu seems frightened. On the same day Caio phones and gives him the same message, using the same words, as if he'd been told what to say. It was a mistake. She was never arrested, never, he stresses. And he rings off without waiting for a reply.

What should he make of the volte-face? It's a charade, clearly. They are lying. A crude charade. They're lying now, not before, when they said she'd been arrested. K feels ill, once again he has that feeling of emptiness; he collapses in the chair. It's over five weeks now. He knows that every day that goes by without news means that his chances of finding her diminish. His thoughts turn to the chemist. Now he knows why he hasn't contacted him yet: he's been infected with the father's disgust at having an informer for a son.

Very early the following day K goes to the chemist. The informer recognises him at once, although K has suddenly begun to look a lot older. He knows that K's daughter's been kidnapped; the whole of Bom Retiro knows. He takes him to the private area they use for injections and there he listens to the old Jew's painful story, with a question added at the end: why did they first tell him she'd been arrested and now deny it?

The chemist knows why but he doesn't say. He starts to talk in general terms, like someone delivering a lecture. He explains that many young Jews have got involved in subversion, and this has revived in the secret services the old myth of the Bolshevik Jew. The Jewish community has got alarmed and has decided to set up a separate group to deal with this, partly because on the government's side too there has been a separation: now the military are in charge of dealing with subversion, with the police playing a secondary role. He carries on talking about the old police issues he knows about, the communists in the cultural centre, the Jews living illegally in the country, Zionist activities in Brazil. None of the channels he uses – friends, family, high-ranking people, exchange of favours – is any use when it comes to subversion, he says.

'There is a rabbi in São Paulo and a community leader in Rio de Janeiro who are in contact with the generals. But, as far as I can tell, that won't help. To give you an idea, not even money works. Not even money, he repeats. There is no escape.'

The chemist writes something on a piece of paper and passes it to K, after all the man was his father's friend: 'Perhaps here they can help you', he says. 'It's close, a shopping arcade, about a hundred metres down there, on the left. Don't tell them who gave you the address.'

The arcade is a narrow two-storey building. They point out the owner to K, a young man in jeans and trainers. K goes up to him and introduces himself, very quickly. The young man is startled but soon recovers. He takes K by the arm and slowly leads him out into the street; he says that the arcade is noisy, they can't talk there. In the street he tells K to walk while he talks; he is listening. He's afraid of being overheard by his employees, K realises. He remembers his daughter's friends, pulling him into the garden at the university.

They walk the length of José Paulino Street and come

back on the other side, K talking, the informer listening. Now and again the informer glances behind him and twice he interrupts K, trying to find out who'd given him the address. But K doesn't let on, he knows it's a test. If he tells him, the informer won't trust him. In the end, the informer asks for K's telephone number and tells him to wait for a call. He can't promise anything but he will try. But don't come back here. I will contact you.

K concludes, from the authoritative way in which the chemist spoke and from the confidence with which the arcade-owner behaved, that Caio and Amadeu were amateurs, who didn't know what they were dealing with. He begins to understand the enigma of the mixed message and he can't stop the knowledge flooding into his distraught mind. He realises, with a pain in his chest, that something so terrible has happened that it frightens people who want to help him, makes them back away – he feels that his daughter has been sucked into an impenetrable system, different from anything he has known, even in Poland. The chemist's explanation impressed him.

Two days later, the arcade-owner phones him. To identify himself he mentions the walk along José Paulino. He tells K that his daughter fled to Portugal more than a month ago. And he rings off. Impossible, thinks K. An ugly lie. His daughter wouldn't make him suffer like this. Even if she couldn't send a message to him in Brazil, she could make contact with their relatives in Israel or with her brother in England, with whom she was in regular touch.

The next week a cylindrical package arrives in his shop by post from Portugal, on which someone has written his daughter's name as the sender. It contains political posters about the Carnation Revolution. He immediately sees that it isn't his daughter's writing: her writing is slightly inclined to the right and regular, with elegant flourishes, just as in a calligraphy exercise. It's a charade. They've put on a charade to torture me. They're all part of the plot, these informers. It's a disgusting network. Damn them all, 'zeln zein ale guein in dred arain', he curses in Yiddish.

He thought back over the information he'd let slip into the treacherous ears of the informers. The most dangerous were the most solicitous, like Caio, who listened right to the end and made promises. K himself had told them where he'd been, who he'd talked to, whether he had important friends, whether he had contacts abroad, which bodies he'd been in touch with, appealing to them to help or to protest, who his lawyer was, who was helping him. And many other pieces of information. 'Ich bin geveinen a groisse idiot', concluded K. I've been a real idiot.

He was still stricken with guilt when his writer and lawyer friend phoned. At the request of the Jewish community leader in Rio de Janeiro, a general would see him. He must seize the chance. He gave him the address and the time. The meeting was to be in the evening. K didn't know if he had any hope left, after so many false leads and after so much time had passed. But the general wouldn't be seeing him to tell him something that a father couldn't bear to hear.

On the arranged evening, as he climbed the white marble steps carved in the shape of petals, which took him to the first floor, K took note of the grandeur of the building, with its neoclassical lines. He suddenly remembered another stairway from another time, in Warsaw, also built in marble in a neoclassical style, which he, still young and strong, had climbed up, taking the steps two at a time, to find out where his sister, Guita, arrested at the rally to launch the party she'd helped to found, the Linke Poalei Zion,[4] was being held. The

4 Literally, the Left of the Party of the Workers of Zion, a left-wing breakaway group from the Poalei Zion, a Zionist party of Marxist orientation created at the beginning of the 20th century in eastern Europe, after the Bund, the Jewish community party, rejected Zionism.

resurfacing of this image, which he thought had been buried beneath the rubble of memory, alarmed him.

K was 30 years old when he was dragged through the streets of Wloclawek,[5] accused of subversion by the Polish police. This was why he'd left the country in a hurry, abandoning his wife and son, who joined him in Brazil a year later. The conditions for his release were a bribe, which his activist friends had funded by pooling resources, and that he leave the country. His sister, Guita, five years older, wasn't so lucky. She'd died from TB in the cold of the prison.

The unexpected image of Guita made him remember how the police officer had sent him back down the stairway in Warsaw, shouting at him that his sister had never been arrested, that she'd fled to Berlin, yes she had, with some lover.

He was still thinking of Guita when he was ushered in to see the general, who received him rudely, brusquely telling him to sit down. He complained that K was spreading heavy and baseless accusations against the military among the Jewish community. And what if his daughter had fled to Buenos Aires with some lover? Had he thought of that?

5   A small town in the west of Poland where the first organised massacre of the Jewish population by German troops took place after the invasion of Poland.

Her first pair of glasses

'It looks nice', said K, looking at her as she put on the glasses.

She didn't say anything, although a careful observer might have noticed a quick twitching of the nerves in her face. It was as if she hadn't heard. She should have brought her friend Sarinha with her when she'd come with her father to order the lenses and choose the frame. It was too late now, she blamed herself.

The girl was 14 years old. She'd just tried on the glasses that she'd chosen with her father the week before. They were her first pair.

Even sitting in the front row, she'd been finding it difficult to read what was written on the blackboard. She'd had to screw up her eyes to make out small letters and numbers. She'd been complaining for some time but her mother hadn't paid any attention.

One day she'd caught the wrong bus and had to walk back eight blocks. She'd misread Vila Diva for Vila Paiva. Only then had her startled father taken her to have her eyes tested. The optician had diagnosed two degrees of myopia in her right eye and one degree in her left.

The girl had asked her mother to go with her to the optician's and help her chose a frame that suited her long and finely defined face. But her mother was tired and had a migraine. She always had migraines. Go with your father, she said.

Since she'd had cancer and had her right breast removed, her mother hardly ever went out. Before then, she'd visited her friends frequently and been proud of her elegant figure, her dark, well-proportioned face, her sculpted, aquiline nose and dark, wavy hair.

Now she only went out some Fridays, using a pad to disguise her mastectomy, but she never visited anyone. She went anonymously to Bom Retiro to buy halva, rye bread or smoked herring. Although she'd lost some of her hair as a result of the chemotherapy, she was still beautiful and elegant.

She was already a sad woman when she'd got pregnant with her daughter, after her two sons. A delegation sent by the Jews in São Paulo to investigate the alarming rumours about what had happened in Poland had come back confirming the worst. Like most Jewish families in Wloclawek, hers had been wiped out. All of them. Her parents, her siblings, her aunts and uncles, her cousins. That, not the blockade, was why they hadn't received any letters after the first days of the German invasion. Not even her cousin Moses had survived, even though he'd escaped to France. The delegation had also confirmed that French Jews had been deported and exterminated. Shortly after she'd heard all this the breast cancer appeared.

At the optician's, the father had chosen a robust and not very expensive frame. Not through miserliness. Not for lack of consideration towards his daughter, his favourite – 'Main teier techterl', my beloved little daughter, he used to say to his friends in the literary circle – but because he didn't have any faith in those delicate Italian frames. Spectacles were to correct your sight. They had to be solid so they didn't break in any little mishap.

His infatuation with his youngest child stopped him from

seeing that she wasn't pretty. When he went to pick her up at school, he used to ask the other students: have you seen the fair-haired girl, the prettiest in the class?

Her classmates smiled indulgently. The girl had angular features, narrow lips and fine, light blonde hair. She was tall and thin. The cleverest in the class certainly, and very popular owing to her warmth and friendliness. But what made her attractive was something quite special that came from within, her spirit, not any doll-like prettiness. All her expressiveness was concentrated in her sad blue eyes, which revealed her immense and restless inner life.

To her father, she was the prettiest girl in the school, whatever glasses she wore. An angel of beauty, he also used to say. In addition, K hadn't had much time the day they went to the opticians. He'd left his partner alone in the shop and it was the beginning of the month, which was always a busy time.

When they got home, the mother was still complaining of her headache.

'How ugly you look', she said. 'Now nothing can be done.'

The daughter didn't reply and her expression didn't change, though an acute observer might perhaps have noticed a quick twitching of the nerves in her face. It was as if she hadn't heard.

The clandestine marriage

When the woman approached him at the meeting of the families of the disappeared and introduced herself – I am your daughter's sister-in-law – K suddenly became aware of just how huge his daughter's other, hidden life had been. She'd even married without him knowing: she'd had a husband, a sister-in-law, parents-in-law. Her husband had also disappeared. Another shock in the never-ending succession of shocks, to discover that another family was also suffering because she'd disappeared, because it had lost not a daughter, but a daughter-in-law, and now he'd have to endure that too, the loss of a son-in-law and the loss of the grandchildren he might have had but now would never have – though he didn't know that yet.

Anxious to find out more, to get to know what this hidden world of hers was like and to meet any friends she might have made in it, he went to the quiet town in the interior of the state where his *machatunes*[1] lived. Clearly she'd often gone there on Sundays.

He discovered that his daughter's partner, the son-in-law he'd never even met, had been mad keen on politics

1   *Machatunes* in the Code of Jewish Law is the relationship that is established between the parents of a married couple.

since he was a small boy. He saw his books, a vast library of revolutionary texts. Through his son-in-law's cousin, who'd helped the couple in their everyday life and thus knew things the rest of the family didn't know, he found out that, although they'd carried on with their normal life, they'd been active in the clandestine struggle against the dictatorship. According to this cousin, the son-in-law belonged to the leadership of one of these organisations. K began to ask himself how they'd got together. Had they got to know each other through politics? Or had they fallen in love first and then decided together to get involved in the armed struggle?

But the question that really tormented him was whether his daughter would have been saved if her husband hadn't been a revolutionary. A moral dilemma: should he hate his son-in-law for having dragged his daughter to a stupid death, or should he honour him for having enriched her life?

And how much was it his son-in-law's fault that she'd got involved in the clandestine struggle? Or had he on the contrary tried to protect her, told her about the risks, tried to keep her out of it, but she'd insisted on supporting him even though she knew it to be dangerous? These questions would never be answered. Even decades afterwards, no one would know precisely how they were kidnapped and killed. Back then, K concluded that the questions didn't make sense. As they'd lived together, there was no way he could have kept her out of it.

When had his daughter got involved? And how? Had it happened gradually, as the couple's life in common had changed almost imperceptibly? Or had they talked it through in depth? Even though it was a family tradition, he'd been surprised to find out about her political militancy; he'd always seen her as a sensitive person, who read poetry, who loved cinema and didn't care much for politics. But once he learnt of her political activism, he understood why she'd been secretive.

Basic rules of safety. He'd also behaved like this when he'd been an activist in Poland. Not only to protect herself and her husband, but mainly to protect him, her father, and her brothers.

But what he couldn't understand was why the marriage had been concealed.

Was it merely because doing things in secret had become a habit? It didn't make sense. For a start, they didn't need to get married. They could have just lived together. Why did they feel they had to make it official? Why had they got married and yet done it secretly?

Both of them had legal lives and stable jobs, their documents were genuine, they had bank accounts and they saved money, while at the same time having this secret political activity, with codenames and hiding places for themselves and the documents they used in their clandestine struggle.

Given that they'd decided to formalise their relationship – for reasons that baffled him – why had they decided to make it part of their secret life, not their legal life? This was a mystery to K. They'd married in secret, as if they were committing a crime, or doing something obscene, or getting involved in yet another conspiracy. Perhaps his cherished daughter was afraid of making him angry if she told him she'd married a goy, a man from a non-Jewish family.

But K was a liberal. His generation had rebelled against religion. They'd pursued the ideals of aufklärung.[2] Although he was Jewish to the marrow, he'd never discriminated in this way. Hadn't his younger son married a Japanese woman? And hadn't his older brother married a Portuguese woman after his first wife died? And hadn't several of his nephews

---

2   Aufklärung – the German name for the Enlightenment – is the name given to a movement of rebellion among eastern European Jewish youth against the stifling religious dogma and rules which their rabbis and elders sought to impose upon every aspect of their lives.

and nieces married non-Jews? And he'd treated them all with equal affection.

Even so, his daughter might have felt afraid to tell him; she was the first woman in the family to marry a non-Jew. Perhaps that was it, as his son-in-law's family had known about the marriage, even though they hadn't made a fuss over it. They'd received her into their family as a beloved daughter-in-law and she'd visited them many times in the interior of the state. K felt mortified when he discovered this.

His daughter had trusted another family, but not him. For them, the marriage hadn't been a secret, just low-key. Was there something bigger behind this? Had she swapped families? The thought hurt him. Was it a response to his marriage to that German woman whom his daughter detested? Or to his intense devotion to Yiddish? A language which neither she nor her brothers could speak – which had also been his fault as he hadn't bothered to teach them.

These thoughts made him feel even guiltier than before.

But none of this explained why they'd married in secret, he mused once again. A secret marriage is a contradiction, a paradox, because the role of marriage is precisely to publicise the formation of a new family, to change the standing of two young people. That's why marriages are such extravagant affairs. If two people didn't want to tell the world about themselves, they needn't get married, they could just live together. It was a mystery.

Perhaps it could all be explained by the pre-nuptial agreement that K had discovered. It established a complete separation of assets between the two. A strangely materialistic concern, for a revolutionary couple. Moreover, it meant they'd already thought about having to separate.

Perhaps they had been foreseeing a time when they would be forced to separate, if one of them was captured by the security services, for instance? That's possible. It makes sense.

Not that they had assets of much value. Their savings and a Beetle. That was all. And the books, of course. All the books.

After mulling it over for a long while, K became convinced that the only reason for them to have married formally in their risky situation was precisely to diminish the risk. How? By having a genuine marriage certificate. With this they could rent a flat without raising eyebrows, they could stay in hotels, or, in an emergency, take refuge in a boarding house without causing suspicion. If necessary, they could even get themselves passports and travel abroad as man and wife, seek exile without anyone suspecting them.

To imagine they could have done this but didn't. That was what hurt most of all.

Letter to a friend

Dearest,

Yesterday I saw again The Exterminating Angel by Buñuel, which we saw together during those good times we had at the Bijou.[1] I'm sure you remember it. It made me want to write to you so much. I hadn't been to the cinema for a long while. In fact, I hardly ever go out nowadays. Though I love cinema, as you know, I've become a recluse. Can you imagine it? After work I go straight home from the chemistry department. I've been avoiding friends. Just going with them for lunch in the biology department. When there's a holiday weekend, we leave São Paulo, go a long way away to where no one knows us. Recently we spent three days in Poços. I remembered that time we went to Paraty. I got all nostalgic. Sometimes I ask myself: why are we doing all this? Maybe it's paranoia but I feel as if we're surrounded by danger. Every day they seize someone on the campus. But, of course, I needn't tell you what's been going on. The atmosphere is very tense. How do we get out of this? I don't know. I just know that what we are doing used to make sense but doesn't any more. That's why Buñuel's film rang true. All those people who could leave but find it impossible to do so, there's no rational explanation. They're held there, as if

---

1   Famous São Paulo art cinema of the 1970s.

in an imaginary prison, and they go to pieces. I never imagined this film would be so relevant for me. I kept asking myself what had inspired Buñuel. Was it the Franco regime or Catholicism or something in his personal life? Whatever it was, it's a wonderful study of what makes people do what they do, what makes them go on walking into a noose, without the strength to change direction. That's what's happening to me. I really wish you were here so I could talk to you. I miss our chats so much. I feel as if the ground is giving way beneath me. I'm no longer able to have fun with my friends at work, except a bit with Celina and Vera. As for the men, I can't bear them, I don't want anything to do with them. They're still the same – the old farts, as you used to call them. They all act as if life is normal, they pretend nothing is happening. My only pleasure nowadays (apart from my great passion but I've already told you about that!) is the little dog that he gave me, a delight. We treat her as if she were our daughter, shampoo her every week, take her for a walk in the park every afternoon. She's called Baleia.[2] It's a homage to Graciliano, of course. She's not a mongrel. She has a pedigree and everything. But I'm even frightened when we take her for these walks. Yet how can we deny her this pleasure? You'd love her. She's a white poodle, with a curly coat. Are you in touch with your brother? I haven't spoken to mine, the one who lives here, for over a year. These people who go to a kibbutz and come back seem all mixed up to me. My brother has decided he's a journalist and that that will protect him. It's just as well that he's going to England in a month or two. I hope he goes soon. I've a horrible feeling that things are going to get a lot worse. I still meet my father once a week or once a fortnight. Since he married again, he's got more affectionate towards me, he wants to please me. I think he needs to cling to me, the last child of that family that he brought up and that doesn't exist any more. At the same time, he's busier than ever with those writer friends of his. I think it's for the

---

2   *Baleia* (whale) is the name of a dog in the novel *Vidas Secas* (Dry Lives) by the famous Brazilian writer Graciliano Ramos.

same reason. The family has ended and all that's left is Yiddish. Can you believe it? They meet every week. There's a woman called Rosa Palatnik whom he treats like a queen, who comes especially from Rio for their meetings. Another who also comes from Rio but less often is Clara Steinberg. Perhaps you've heard of them? I really don't know if they're good writers or not. But woe betide anyone who interrupts one of their meetings! I don't know what it's like in Rio but what strikes me most here is how alienated people are. I'm not talking about those old farts in the chemistry department, but about other people, people I respect. They seem fatalistic, cold, as if they've lost their humanity, as if politics were everything and nothing else mattered. Some are also very arrogant. It seems as if people are creating their own worlds, outside the real world, shutting themselves up. And that's the case for both the old farts and for clear-headed and engaged people. Something very wrong and truly horrible is happening. A situation with no way out and with no rational explanation, just as in Buñuel's film. There's an unbearable tension and no hope of anything. I don't know any more what's a lie and what's the truth. The worst of all is that I haven't anyone to talk to, except my love, and he is precisely one of the most inflexible. By the way, neither my brother nor my father knows we got married. My father doesn't know anything about my life. There's a reason for all this. I would really, really love to see you but, if you come to São Paulo, don't try to find me, leave a message with one of our friends and I'll find a way to contact you. And please don't send me a reply through the post, not even to my father's address. Whatever happens, remember I love you a lot.

A big hug

A.

Books and revolution

I

He stole books. His briefcase had a hidden partition which made it easy. He took everything: philosophical tracts, treatises on political economy, history books, biographies, novels; but he preferred the classics of Marxism. One by one he got hold of the complete works of Marx and Engels and the main texts of Caio Prado, Leôncio Basbaum, Celso Furtado, Josué de Castro and Ignácio Rangel.[1] He also filched books about the evils of imperialism and the justice of the freedom struggles in Africa and Asia.

He knew all the bookshops and second-hand bookshops in São Paulo, even the most difficult to find, those hidden inside buildings or not visible from the street. He went to them regularly, and every second or third visit he bought a book to keep up appearances. The booksellers regarded him as a good customer, though they must have noticed that he bought only the cheapest books. They probably thought he was poor.

1 These writers are some of Brazil's most important scholars and thinkers, mostly Marxists.

In fact, although he wasn't well-off, he wasn't poor. He studied at university in the evenings, and during the day he worked in computer programming, a skill that he'd learnt easily and one that wasn't very common in those days, so it paid well. He had a high IQ and was well-informed; he read most of the books he stole.

He could have paid for the books but he stole them on principle. He was expropriating them in the name of the socialist revolution, he explained to the few people he confided in. It was as if he was practising the subversion that was preached in some of the Marxist texts; each expropriation was sabotaging the market that had turned ideas into a means of making money. He was a Bakunin, an enemy of private property, a revolutionary acquiring an arsenal for the great assault on power. He thought it educational and stimulating to be in a state of permanent transgression.

He also knew the semi-illegal bookshops of the Communist Party, the Socialist Party and the two wings of the Trotskyist movement – the Lambertian and the Fourth International. But he didn't expropriate books from them. He was a revolutionary, not a thief.

His dominant feature was his jutting jaw, which gave him a determined and intransigent look. He seemed like a war veteran, although he was young, a student. He never told amusing stories, though he frequently smiled that ironic smile of someone who knows he's superior. It was as if he felt himself better than ordinary people because he was convinced of the role he would play in the coming revolution. And, unlike his colleagues, who also called themselves rebels and socialists but did nothing, he devoted a huge amount of time to preparing for the revolution. His passion for revolution was matched only by his love of books.

II

On the day the military went into the streets, suspending civil rights, when left-wing activists were scared and apprehensive, this young man resolutely contacted one of his confidants who had a car for a special mission.

With cold-blooded calculation they visited the left-wing parties' offices and bookshops, knowing they'd been abandoned in a hurry. They went to them one after another, not missing out a single one.

Methodically, they collected the books, pamphlets, newspapers, anything they could find, just like someone removing arms from an arsenal so they won't fall into enemy hands. They even removed the list of party members they found in the Socialist Party office.

III

Some time later, after he'd been seized and disappeared by the military, the only thing of value that he left behind was his revolutionary library of over 2,000 volumes, most of them expropriated. Strangely, he had written in firm and rapid handwriting his full name and the date of the expropriation on the flyleaf of each of them.

Was he claiming ownership? No. It can't have been that. Perhaps he knew – and had always known – that these books would be all that would survive of his revolutionary career, tiny headstones for a tomb that still doesn't exist.

Jacobo

I

Sitting with his back to the wall, K looks around the coffee shop, his gaze resting, one by one, on everyone there. He feels as if he's in an American film, and realises for the first time just how realistic these films are. The fellow with a felt hat on the back of his head reading a newspaper in Yiddish can only be Jewish; the man in a hurry with a briefcase is clearly a lawyer; and there is the Italian-looking taxi driver, still wearing a cap. The America of European immigrants is in this coffee shop.

It distresses him to realise that there he is, thinking of American films when he's only in New York for one reason – to find out what's happened to his daughter. But he can't help thinking that, instead of ending up in Brazil, he could have been one of these immigrants. Who knows, perhaps if he'd gone to North America like his cousin Simon, not to South America, this tragedy wouldn't have happened.

Twenty years earlier he'd gone to New York to receive a prize for his poem 'Haguibor', published in the magazine *Tzukunft*.[1]

---

[1] A Yiddish literary magazine published in New York. 'Tzukunft' means the future in Yiddish; 'Haguibor' means a strong and fearless man.

On the surface very little had changed since then. But three of New York's five Yiddish newspapers had closed down. How can a language disappear so quickly? The Germans had killed its readers and Stalin had killed its writers: he is repeating to himself what he never tires of saying in his talks back home.

Ah, if he hadn't spent all his time thinking about Yiddish, about literature, if he'd paid more attention to his daughter, to his sons ... But now, there he was, sipping a weak coffee, waiting for the office of the American Jewish Committee to open. They had said they would see him at 9 a.m.

II

The building reflects the might of the Morgans and the Rockefellers, it's the America of the steel and oil fortunes. On the way in, he stops as he notices a bronze plaque in memory of the young Jewish girls from very poor families who'd arrived in America having been promised husbands, and who'd finished up having to work as prostitutes: the *polacas*,[2] as they called them in Brazil. A sudden thought: the Jews in Bom Retiro hadn't had the decency to erect a memorial like this one.

Irineu Blaumstein, an elderly man, perhaps about his own age, receives him. They talk in Yiddish. Blaumstein says he knows him through his stories and poems, published in New York magazines. K tells him about the disappearance of his daughter and son-in-law. He gives him a sheet of paper containing all the information. And some photographs. He doesn't know who else to turn to, he explains in a beseeching tone. He's just come from London, where he met Amnesty International. Before that, he'd been in Geneva, where he'd met the Red Cross. He asks politely why the American Jewish

2 *Polaca* means Polish woman in Portuguese.

Committee hasn't publicly criticised the Brazilian dictatorship, as Amnesty International has done.

What has Amnesty International done? asks Blaumstein.

They've launched an international campaign, says K. They've asked their members to send protest letters to the Brazilian government; his daughter had been chosen as 'political prisoner of the year'.

As he talks of the dictatorship, K recalls with disgust the Human Rights Commission at the Organisation of American States, which had cynically turned down his request for help. It said it had been informed by the Brazilian government that it had no information about his daughter. It was obvious what had happened: they'd asked the thugs if they were thugs. As for the Red Cross, they'd taken down all the information and said they would start a search. But they didn't seem to expect much from their Brazilian section.

Amnesty had suggested that he ask for help from the American Jewish Committee, K said. They'd told him that this Committee had a lot of experience in these cases and was very influential in high-level American circles. The Red Cross had also praised the Jewish Committee.

Blaumstein then explains to K how the American Jewish Committee operates in the human rights sphere. Since it was founded in 1906, with the aim of doing something about the pogroms in Russia, it had sought to promote pluralism and to eradicate prejudice, believing this to be the best way to combat anti-Semitism, seeing it as part of a broader problem of intolerance and discrimination.

As far as particular cases like that of his daughter were concerned, the American Jewish Committee had learnt over time that the best tactic was to work silently, behind the scenes; that was how they did things. To tell the truth, he says, Amnesty International also uses two tactics, one very public and the other much more discreet, though they do

47

it differently from the Committee. Many people have been saved in this way. You have no idea of our ability to reach people in high positions, says Blaumstein.

He asks K where he is staying. In my cousin Simon's house in Brooklyn, says K, writing the address on the piece of paper with the information about his daughter. Blaumstein tells him to expect some news by, at the latest, midday the following day. He recommends secrecy in his contacts with the Committee. Discretion is crucial, he insists.

On the following day, well before midday, a courier arrives at his cousin Simon's house with an envelope for K which contains the message: 'You will be contacted in São Paulo shortly by Jacobo. He has an Argentine accent and will tell you he wants to talk to you about your new book of poetry. Memorise this message and destroy this piece of paper.'

Remarkable, thinks K, that such respectable bodies, such powerful bodies, humanitarian organisations, need to behave secretly, as if they were criminals; it almost seems as if they too are afraid of being disappeared. It's as if malefactors who disappear people are active everywhere. Even in America, the land of freedom. That night he returns to São Paulo.

III

Just over two weeks go by.

Then K receives a phone call from Sr Jacobo, who wants to talk to him about his proposal for a new book of poems. He speaks a bit in Yiddish and a bit in Portuguese, with an Argentine accent. They arrange to meet in the library at the Hebrew Club. Jacobo asks him to bring all the original copies of his poems and, if he has any drafts, to bring them too.

K once again gathers all the information and the photographs. He takes with him too some original poems in

Yiddish, just in case he has to put on an act. Jacobo welcomes him effusively in the library café, just as an editor would treat a great poet whose work he is about to publish.

Jacobo is young, about 30 years old, with a full head of blond hair. He seems like a serious person who feels he must appear jovial. More of a sportsman arriving for a tennis match than an editor on a business trip.

They exchange compliments as they stand at the bar, and then settle themselves in one of the partitioned areas in the library and start to talk openly, but lowering their voices. They speak at times in Yiddish, at times in Portuguese.

Jacobo interrogates K for three hours: he wants to know everything. His daughter's and son-in-law's militancy, the names of the people he's already spoken to. He insists on dates and places. Above all, dates. He says the date of the disappearance is key for knowing who to speak to and for finding out what happened. He spends a lot of time going through K's contacts with the authorities, people in government, lawyers and the Catholic archdiocese. He says they are dealing with a quite extraordinary plan for making people disappear without leaving any trace at all.

It's not difficult to make bodies disappear, says Jacobo – in Argentina, for instance, they threw them from a plane into the sea a long way from the coast – but there's always someone who saw something, a pilot, an underling who transported the bodies.... Then he notices the despair in K's eyes and changes his tone: his organisation had found almost a hundred Jews and some non-Jews, thought to have been disappeared, who were being secretly held. They'd obtained safe conducts for them with entry visas to Israel, where some of them had stayed. Others had travelled on to Europe and the United States. Who knows? Perhaps they could achieve something like that for his daughter and son-in-law?

Don't despair, he told K. There's still hope. Thousands of

people have been disappeared in Argentina – he says – perhaps more than ten thousand, and they are still kidnapping and disappearing people, but suddenly someone they'd lost hope for is found, almost miraculously. He'd had a lot of experience with the disappeared and he promised to make good use of it in the search for his daughter. The story of the old Jew, a writer and poet, suddenly overwhelmed by what has been done to his daughter, deeply moves people, he says. Finally, they part. He promises to send news. He tells K not to lose hope.

IV

Two months go by and nothing from Jacobo. At the end of October, K receives a phone call from someone called Carlos, who talks about how preparations are proceeding for his next book of poetry. Just like Jacobo, he has a strong Argentine accent. We need to talk about the book, Carlos says.

They meet in the same private section of the Hebrew library. Carlos was already waiting for K, who'd taken a taxi, not from the taxi rank by the baker's next to his house, but picking one up in the street. As an extra precaution, he'd got it to put him down not at the door of the library, but a bit further away, by a residential block.

Carlos tells K that, despite all their efforts, they haven't been able to get any reliable information about his daughter. It's as if an insurmountable wall has been built around her and her husband. On two occasions, he says, someone had admitted that she'd been detained, but at a second meeting soon after they'd said they'd made a mistake. And they hadn't been able to find out anything at all about her husband. He wanted to know if K had new information, a new lead.

K says no. Nothing. Deeply depressed, he scarcely hears

what Carlos is saying. He feels very tired. Once again that feeling of inner emptiness that stops him even getting up from his chair. He thinks back to Jacobo, so full of energy and optimism that he'd made K feel that there might be a chance.

'And how's Jacobo?' he asks.

'That's why I came, and not him,' says Carlos. '"Jacobo disappeared two months ago. We're very worried. He disappeared without trace.'

The dog

What can we do with this damned dog? We did a bloody good job with the couple, didn't we, just as the boss likes it. Covered our tracks. No one saw us, nothing went wrong, fucking brilliant we were. We didn't even go into the house, that house that was so close to the others, damn close to the others, right on top of the neighbours. But we surprised the two of them, down that alleyway. It was a stroke of luck for us, that side exit from the park, half hidden from sight. By the time the two realised what was happening they were in the car, a sack over their heads. Only that bloody dog barked, but by then it was too late. In the end we had to take the wretched bitch with us, that damned dog, we had no choice, and now it's a real pain in the arse. We hadn't thought of the dog. Lima had taken care of everything – smartarse, he even knew the name of the dog, Baleia (whale), a stupid name for a tiny little bitch with ridiculous long hair. Where did they get the name from? I asked Lima if he was sure it was right. He said of course it was right, it was in his report. He's always doing that, being a clever dick. He thinks he's so clever. But it doesn't help, calling the dog by her name, she pays no attention. She hasn't eaten since she arrived, she just takes a sip of water now and again, that's all. She hasn't eaten for six days but she won't fucking die, she just stays where she is, flopped out on the floor, ears drooping. If we go close, she snarls, the bitch, as if she's accusing us, as if she knows everything. The only thing that gets her going is the door opening. Then she's awake in a trice. Long before the door opens she knows what's happening, she jumps up, her ears pricked. She thinks it's her owners and when she realises it's not, she collapses in a heap. She's always like that, she leaps up, full of life, then she collapses. Stupid cunt, doesn't she know they're never going to come back? How can dogs be so clever and so stupid at the same time? It should have been in the report that the couple took their dog with them on their walks in the park. The fact is that Lima forgot to put it in, that's the truth, Lima who's so proud of never forgetting anything. But he says it's our fucking fault. We only had to put two and two together. If the couple had a dog and they always went for a walk in the park in the afternoons, it was damn obvious, he says, that the walk was for the dog, so that she could run around and do her business. There he is, at it again, taking the piss out of us. And the bastard didn't fucking tell us that it was a stuck-up little dog, the kind that fancy women have. I don't get it – two terrorists having a dog like this. Perhaps they weren't fucking terrorists at all. It doesn't make sense. Or perhaps they got the dog as a cover, so that we wouldn't suspect them. Or perhaps she was a watchdog. Her hearing is bloody good, isn't it? Perhaps she warned them if a stranger was breaking into the house. Well, she fucking well messed it up this time, didn't she? She took too fucking long, didn't she? She didn't bark in time. I wonder if she feels guilty? We're never going to know; anyway, we're going to kill this bitch straightaway. There's nothing else we can do. The damned dog doesn't stop whining at night. It's driving us mad. She seems to do it on purpose to keep us awake. I don't understand the boss, he's a real tough bastard, but when I tell him the dog's a problem, she's a danger for us, he pretends not to hear. He's always going on at us, wants to be sure we didn't leave any tracks, that no one saw us. He wants to be fucking certain that no one will ever know that we made off with them. But when I talk about the dog, warn him that she could give us away, that a friend of theirs could recognise her and that would fuck everything up, then he doesn't want to know. I told him that that the damn dog hadn't eaten anything since she arrived and he blamed me, saying I must have given the wrong food to the dear little doggie, even sent me off to buy expensive meat, more expensive than steak! He was even worse yesterday. When I said we had to get rid of her, he swore at me, said I was a brute, a coward, that anyone who hurts a dog is a coward. I almost said to him: and what about those who are fucking killing these poor students? Aren't they much more of a brute than me? Those students have mums and dads like the rest of us, and they wouldn't harm anyone locked away. And, worse still, what about those who are cutting them up into bits so they can get rid of them, make them disappear without trace, what about them? I got that fucking close to saying something. Thank God I didn't. I must have been out of my fucking mind. I don't know what I was thinking. But we've still got this damned dog. It doesn't give me any rest. It's OK for the boss. He only comes here when new prisoners arrive. Fresh meat, he calls them. He gets what he can from them, then he says it's time to get rid of them and off he goes. But we're here the whole time, with this dog tormenting us, but I know what I'm going to do. I'll give it a couple of days, then if she doesn't die by herself I'll put poison in her water, the poison we gave that politician.

The day the Earth stood still

K is glued to the radio, others are waiting for the television transmission; a group of mothers and sisters has gathered under the large, flashing news panel on the front of the offices of the morning daily, the *Estado de S. Paulo*. They're like stargazers, anxiously waiting for the century's only eclipse of the moon. But, instead of clutching telescopes, their common bond is hope. The President has said that, at midday precisely, the justice minister, Armando Falcão, will tell them what has happened to the disappeared.

As the moment approaches, it is as if the sun has come to a standstill, the breeze has expired, the world has halted. A taboo had been broken. The government will speak about the disappeared, so hope has been reborn. Six months earlier, the Archbishop of São Paulo had published a list of twenty-two disappeared people. The newspapers had reproduced it discreetly, fearing the rage of the unpredictable censor.

The moment arrives. At midday the transmission begins. Soon the names are given, in alphabetical order of first names. His daughter should be one of the first but her name isn't on the list. Others, listening carefully, are dumbfounded by what they're being told. This person is known to have left the country, that one was never detained, the next one has left the country too. Another person has been released, after completing his sentence.

Suddenly, the name of a respected economics lecturer is mentioned as having disappeared, a man who was never arrested, although he was expelled from the university, and who goes on living where he's always lived and seeing the friends he's always seen. And so it goes on, with other derisory accounts. Instead of twenty-two explanations, twenty-seven lies. And then, finally, a reference to his daughter. There's no record of her, her husband, and two others in the official documents.

Psychological warfare has dictated the way in which the military have carried out the President's promise. In this kind of war, it is legitimate to confuse your enemy with lies, which have the same function as smokescreens in conventional warfare. Those who'd hoped for a humanitarian account of what had happened to the victims in a war the military had already won were completely wrong-footed. On the contrary, the false list became an effective arm in a new strategy of psychological warfare. It would have been better for us if they hadn't said anything, K concludes.

Once the list has been read out, the special broadcast from the justice ministry comes to an end. After a few seconds, the earth resumes its orbit and the breeze blows again. People turn away. But K doesn't move. He feels weary.

Psychological warfare

'What can they do to you that they haven't already done?'
Moises Ibn Ezra

I

Mineirinho, get Fogaça from the cell. I'm going to do this bastard over and then let him go. Tell the guards he's leaving. Tell him to get ready, collect his things. These cunts think I'm frightened of the big names. But, fuck it all, I'm not afraid of any of them. Not of that cunt Golbery,[1] who's pretending he's a saint, not of the President of the Republic, not of the Pope, not of this fucking American senator. I don't give a shit about any of them. They told me, didn't they, to do what it takes to wipe out the communists? And I wiped them out, didn't I? So now they can't complain. It all started when that old man spoke to the senator, gave him a letter – but I don't give a damn about the fuckers.

II

Fogaça, sit down! For fuck's sake, sit down! Now listen – why are you shaking? For fuck's sake, stop it. You're going to do a

---

1 The reference is to General Golbery do Couto e Silva, one of the main leaders of the 1964 military coup, who later masterminded a gradual and military-controlled transition to democracy.

little job for me. If you do it properly, I'll let set you free. Got it? You're going to take this phone here and dial the number I give you. An old man will answer and you're going to tell him your name, your real name. You're going to tell him the Dops[2] has just released you and that you saw his daughter when you were inside. The old fucker's going to go mad, he'll jump up and down, he'll ask a lot of questions, how's his daughter and so on, you say nothing, just say you saw her and she gave you his number. Now this is what you do, you cunt. You say you're in the bus station near the Dops, that you're phoning from the bus station, that you're just about to leave. That you've only got enough money to pay for the fare to Tatuí, that your family lives in Tatuí. The old man's going to say he must see you, you say you can't, you have to leave. Then he'll tell you to get a taxi to his house and he'll pay, or he may say that he will pick you up. Say that he must come and pick you up. Make the fucker come and pick you up. Say you'll wait by the chemist's near the bus station. But tell him to come soon. Ask him what his car's like. Have you got all that, you bastard? You do it properly and I'll let you go. If you fuck it up, back into the cell with you. I'll put you in solitary. Mineirinho, dial the number for him and pass him the phone. The cunt's trembling so much he's fucking useless.

III

Mineirinho, you saw how well it worked out with Fogaça? Only it's not what you think, Mineirinho. The old fucker didn't come because he believed what I said. He's too canny for that. He came because he couldn't not come. He had to come, do you get it? Mineirinho, that's what's clever about

<hr />

2   Department of Political and Social Order (DOPS) was the name of the political police during the military dictatorship.

it, the psychology. He had to come, even though he didn't believe a word of it. And do you know why? Why he's chasing after these high-up people, even after all this time? It's because he can't accept that his daughter has copped it. He refuses to accept it. So he grasps at anything, even knowing it's a trap. The fucker couldn't not go, not try. Know something, Mineirinho? It was a great idea of mine.

IV

Mineirinho, you remember that old man we fucked up by getting Fogaça to pretend he'd seen his daughter? Well, damn it all, the old man still hasn't given up. We're going to have to be even smarter. Get his address from the file, while I phone Rocha in Lisbon. There's a three-hour time difference. We've still got time.

V

Is that the consul? Get Rocha for me, please. Tell him it's Fleury.

It that you, Rocha? Is everything OK? I need you to do something for me. Get hold of some of those leaflets about that stupid carnation revolution, that nonsense, and mail them to the address Mineirinho will give you. Put them in a packet and send them, by airmail. Don't include a message, just put the address and the name of the sender on the back. Write it. Write it in a girl's handwriting. Mineirinho, give him the old man's address and the girl's full name. He's going to go mad again. The bastard. If they hadn't told us to stop everything, I'd kill one of these old people, just to get the rest to stop. I'd kill him or that snobbish cunt Zuzu, who keeps stirring things up in the States.

VI

Mineirinho, they've delivered the package Rocha sent from Lisbon. Lima checked with the Post Office. The old bastard must be reeling. And now comes the killer blow. You phone our man in Bom Retiro, the man in the arcade, and tell him the girl is going to arrive in Guarulhos[3] from Portugal tomorrow morning on a TAP flight. Lima's checked there's a flight tomorrow. This will really do him in. I'm beginning to get angry with this fucking Jew. He can mess things up for us. So we'll get him to go there. Watch everyone arrive, one by one, slowly. And not a fucking sign of his daughter, of course. We're going to wear him out, get him so stressed he has a heart attack, the cunt.

VII

The bosses have sent us another message, Mineirinho. Things are getting nasty, there's a lot of people getting involved, putting on pressure. That report from Lima about the meeting the Archbishop had with the relatives is fucking worrying too. Now it's not just this old fucker and that Zuzu cunt and a few others, now it's become political. It's becoming a fucking movement. And the cunts up there talking about an 'opening'. Is it the right time to be opening up? It's fucking obvious we've got to wait. We've only just finished the job.

We've got to change everything, Mineirinho. The enemy now are the terrorists' families. We've got to be clever, use psychology, Mineirinho. We've got to wear these families down through psychology.

Do the following, Mineirinho. Phone one of the fuckers on the families' commission, it can be anyone on the list Lima

3   São Paulo's principal international airport.

prepared. Phone and tell him some of the disappeared women have been locked away in the Juqueri madhouse.[4] Say that the damn chemistry lecturer is one of them and that there are others but you don't know their names. Say you know because you worked in Juqueri. And then ring off. Don't give him time to ask anything. Got it, Mineirinho?

VIII

Mineirinho, I knew we only had to wait. It took a week but it worked. I knew they'd take the bait, that the old man would find out. It seems he went alone to Franco da Rocha, went straight there, knocked on the door and said he wanted to see his daughter. You're saying no, he didn't go alone? He went with two others? So they're acting as a group now? It's all as we thought. They must have all got frazzled, the cunts, trying to work out how to get into Juqueri, trying to find a doctor, or someone who works for the Judicial Asylum, to help them. We'll just wait for all the fuckers to wear themselves out with this business.

IX

Lima says that it's run its course, this Juqueri thing, now that it's been going on for two months. They're giving up. He says they're sniffing around the mortuary now. The old man's been there, with some others. They won't discover anything but it's not good, them going there; the fuckers are getting too close to some of our schemes. Thinking about it, Mineirinho, we

---

4   Juqueri hospital in Franco da Rocha is the largest hospital in São Paulo for the mentally ill. It is notorious for the terrible conditions in which the inmates are kept. The word Juqueri has come to mean a madhouse.

need to be a step ahead all the time and it's time we used our people abroad again. Lurdes, in Ottawa, she's good. Tell her to phone this old cunt and tell him she's seen his daughter. She can invent a story. She can say she's a Brazilian tourist and a fair-haired girl heard her speaking Portuguese, introduced herself and gave her her father's phone number. She was so moved by the story that she decided out of the goodness of her heart to phone from there, before she came back. Lurdes will do it well, she'll enjoy it.

X

Mineirinho, we're doing something wrong. The bastards haven't given up. Mineirinho, you'll never believe it, the old man has managed to get Kissinger involved! Mineirinho, don't you know who Kissinger is? He's the bloke that started all this business. An American, as clever as they come. Only the situation has changed there and is changing here too. This damned 'opening'. Know what we're doing wrong, Mineirinho? We shouldn't be stringing them along, keeping them hoping against hope they'll find them alive in Juqueri or abroad. The cunts know we're tricking them but they let themselves be tricked. And we encourage them. But now we've fucking well got to do the opposite. We can tire the cunts out in the same way or even more by getting them to think the relatives they're looking for are dead and buried first in one place and then in another. To hunt for someone alive is one thing but to hunt for a body just so you can bury it is different. It'll do their fucking heads in. Come on, Mineirinho. I'm a genius, aren't I? Not even Falcão thought of this.

XI

So that's what we'll do, Mineirinho, we'll fucking well invent rumours about where the bodies are. One rumour after another. We'll invent one rumour, wait a while, one or two months, and then invent another. We'll really wear the cunts out, get them to drop down dead. That uncle of yours, Mineirinho, who has a steakhouse in Ibiúna, is he still an estate agent? Mineirinho, ask him to find a large property, one with high walls. One that's empty, if possible. You take down the address and pass it on to the families just as you did with Juqueri. But now it's corpses they're searching for, not living people. Don't give them the full address, just more or less where it is and a few hints. Let the fuckers think they've found the house themselves.

XII

Mineirinho, sit down. Something strange is happening. I don't like it one bit. Do you know who came to see me? Robert, that bloke from the CIA. Can you believe it? That fucking old man has won over someone in the CIA in the States. Robert says he's been told by Washington to find the girl and her husband. An order from the States, Mineirinho. This old man with his fucking little shop in Tucuruvi. He's got more clout than he pretends or he's got important relatives in the States. Just as well that Robert warned me. Mineirinho, he wants to make a deal, we hand over the girl and her husband and they take our names off all their documents. You know what it's like there, don't you, Mineirinho? One damn day these documents will be leaked to the press and we'll be completely fucked. Robert says everything has changed. That it's time to clean up the archives, destroy all the evidence. As if I didn't know. But hand over the girl? What a fucking stupid idea! Even if they were alive, we fucking well couldn't hand them over after all that's happened. Much better to destroy all the evidence. But we've done that. Long before they told us to. You have to admit it, Mineirinho, compared with me, the Americans are pathetic, just amateurs.

The matzeiva

'What you are asking is absurd, to put up a matzeiva[1] when there isn't a body…'

The rabbi is emphatic. K chose him because he belongs to the modern faction. Who knows, not being orthodox, he will perhaps allow a headstone for his daughter to be put up beside his wife's tomb in the Jewish cemetery in Butantã. But the rabbi turns down his request; what's more, he shows no sympathy at all for K's terrible situation.

This will change a few months later, when another rabbi, with even more modern views, arrives from the United States and agrees to officiate at the ecumenical service for the Jewish journalist assassinated by the military. K is simply a little ahead of his time.

'There isn't a single word in all of the Talmud[2] nor in the fourteen books of the Mishneh Torah that speaks of a matzeiva without a corpse', says the rabbi. And he continues as if he were lecturing: 'What is a burial but giving back to the earth what came from the earth? Adam, adama, man and earth, the same word; the body slowly decomposes and the soul is slowly set free; that's why we forbid cremations and embalming, why

---

1 A tombstone with an inscription. It is generally erected a year after the burial.
2 The traditional compendium of Jewish religious law.

we forbid the use of metal coffins and of nails to fasten down the coffin lid, and why we have so many other prohibitions. There's simply no sense in a burial without a body.'

K doesn't need this lesson from the rabbi. While still a child in the heder,[3] he studied all the books on Jewish rites, even the book of Zohar.[4] He certainly knows Hebrew better than any rabbi in São Paulo. Although he has rejected religion, he knows its precepts; he knows that a tombstone should be erected a year after the death when, according to the gaonim,[5] the wise men, the memory of the dead person becomes more vivid.

K suddenly understands with unexpected intensity why this custom is right: now that it's a year since he lost his daughter, he feels the urgent need to put up a tombstone for her. Not to have an inscription is like saying that she never existed, and that's not true: she existed, became an adult, developed a personality, created her world, graduated, married. Not to be able to erect a tombstone feels like a further disaster, an additional punishment for his alienation and his failure to see what was happening to his daughter under his nose.

'Without a body, there's no ritual, there's nothing', continues the rabbi. 'There's no tahara,[6] no purification of the body. And why do we wash the body? Because only purified bodies can lie in a Jewish cemetery.'

Does the rabbi mean that my daughter wasn't pure? What does he know about my daughter? Nothing. For K the rabbi is mouthing empty words. They'd already told him in the Burial Society, the Chevra Kadisha, that a matzeiva wasn't possible without a body. He'd retorted to Avrum, the secretary of the

3 Jewish primary school, generally headed by a rabbi, which uses the Torah as its main text.
4 A collection of the five books of the Kabbalah, with mystical commentaries about the Torah and the origin of the universe.
5 The spiritual leaders who emerged during the exile in Babylon and, by extension, the wisest of the wise.
6 Obligatory rite for the washing of the body before it is buried.

society, that in the entrance to the cemetery at Butantã there's a large tombstone with an inscription in memory of those who died in the Holocaust, and there are no bodies beneath it. Avrum had admonished him for comparing what had happened to his daughter to the Holocaust. Nothing compared with the Holocaust, he'd said. He'd been so angry he'd got up to go. There's only one Holocaust, it's unique, absolute evil. K agreed with this but said that for him his daughter's tragedy was a continuation of the Holocaust. And he argued that in Eretz Israel[7] it is common to add the names of relatives killed in the Holocaust to a dead person's matzeiva. This reference to the custom in Eretz Israel was decisive: the secretary gave in but, as it was going to be the first time something like this had ever happened, he'd asked K to get a rabbi to back the action. So K has gone to see the 'modern' rabbi, who continues with his lecture.

'Placing the matzeiva is the last act in the burial so that relatives and friends can pay their respects to the dead person and say a kaddish[8] for the salvation of his or her soul. What's the origin of the matzeiva? Why did our ancestors place it there? It was put there so that tombs wouldn't be desecrated, so that bodies wouldn't be violated. And so we return to the original question: if there's no body, there's nothing to desecrate, there's nothing to violate. There's no reason for putting a matzeiva.'

K is scarcely listening. Angry, he's feeling once again what he thought about rabbis' knowledge when he was young, that it's a medieval word game without any relevance to what's going on in the world. These same rabbis had done nothing

---

7   It was the term used before the creation of the State of Israel to refer to the territory of the State of Israel and the Palestinian territories. The term is still used.
8   The main prayer in the Jewish rite recited during a burial by the oldest son or the closest relative.

when he turned to them for help. Even the Archbishop of São Paulo had attempted something, but these rabbis, nothing.

'It's also forbidden to bury the bad with the good. And there are many other rules, as you know. Maimonides thought that those who'd married non-Jews should not be buried on sacred ground. And that people who'd committed suicide should not be buried on sacred ground, but close to the wall.'

Before he'd hinted that she wasn't pure; now he's talking about suicide. What does he know? Absolutely nothing. Or is he suggesting she wasn't a good Jew because she'd married a goy? They'd used this kind of argument when they'd refused to allow *polacas* (Polish prostitutes) to be buried in the Vila Mariana cemetery; those poor women, who weren't criminals, just poor Jews who'd been deceived by the mafia – a shameful story that no one wanted to talk about. They'd had to create their own cemetery, a long way away in Chora Menino. The *polacas* in Santos had faced the same problem.

The rabbi continues with his lecture: 'The cemetery also has the educational function of reminding us that, when the angel of death seeks us out, we're all equal; that's why the tombstones have to be modest, with a simple inscription with the name of the dead person, the dates on which he or she died and was born, and the names of the father and mother.'

K isn't convinced. Would the community have been so indifferent to what had happened to his daughter if she'd been a Klabin or a Safra?[9] No. The community, this rabbi and even perhaps the scoundrels in government would have reacted quite differently. Thoroughly depressed but resolute, K said goodbye somewhat brusquely and walked rapidly towards the stairs. The rabbi's last remarks followed him out:

'What you're really after is a monument that pays homage to your daughter, not a tombstone, not a matzeiva. But she

9 Both the Safra and the Klabin are rich Jewish families well-known in Brazil.

was a terrorist, wasn't she? And you want our community to pay homage to a terrorist on our sacred ground? You want to put us at risk because of a terrorist? For a communist? For that was what she was, wasn't she?'

The same accusation, also expressed as a question in exactly the same words, had been made a month earlier by a Jewish millionaire, the owner of a TV network and a friend of former presidents and generals. K had spoken to him at the suggestion of another important Jew. He'd told him the story of his daughter in the hope that he'd find something out through his friends the generals. The Jewish millionaire had listened impatiently and then asked a question, which showed he thought that what had happened to K's daughter was justified, and that it was pointless to continue the conversation: 'But wasn't she a communist?' K had responded immediately: 'She was a lecturer at the University of São Paulo.'

It then occurred to K, who was feeling wretched at his failure with the matzeiva, that he could put together a small book in memory of his daughter and his son-in-law. A tombstone in the form of a book. A book in memoriam. They had done this from time to time in Poland, though there it hadn't been a substitute for the matzeiva. He would put together an album of eight or ten pages, with photographs and testimonies from their friends. He would have a hundred copies printed and then distribute them by hand to all the family members, and to their colleagues and friends; he would send it to his relatives in Israel.

It was more work than he'd expected. The testimonies had to be collected and then typed up; then there was the question of the layout, of deciding the order of the texts and the photos. His daughter's friends helped, because K knew how to write correctly only in Hebrew and Yiddish. They all gave testimonies and one of them did the layout for him. On the first page they decided to put that beautiful picture of her on her graduation day.

Once this work was done, K went to a small local printers', which had once been owned by an Italian anarchist, called Ítalo, a former customer now deceased, with whom K had sometimes exchanged ironic political observations. K always preferred local tradesmen. In the past, the printers had produced a small anarchist newspaper called *Labor*. Now in the son's hands, it printed wedding invitations, visiting cards and tax receipts.

On the following day, K returned to find out how much it would cost and when it would be ready. The young man almost shouted at him when he arrived:

'How dare you bring subversive material into my shop? Take it back and get out! Never show your face here again with anything similar. Just think of it, bringing me subversive material, about a disappeared person, a terrorist. She was a communist, wasn't she?'

Left in the lurch

When we start feeling the pains of old age, the right thing is for our children to look after us, right to the end, and then to bury us. Then for the children of our children to do the same for them, and so it goes on. But I don't know what's going to happen to us. You, sir, have your little shop, your daughter used to talk about it, but what do we have? The pension the missus gets isn't much; and I don't even get that. He was the first in the family to go to college, hard-working he was, he had a job during the day and studied at night. He earned well. At the end of every month, he'd turn up here, pick up the bills, electricity, water, whatever we hadn't paid; and he'd go to the village shop and the butcher's, pay off what we'd had on tick. This little house of ours, he sorted out the paperwork, made the monthly payment, took all the bother off our shoulders. Our youngest, the girl, she helps but she can't do much. She's on her own, has her daughter to look after. The missus's hair went white overnight, it hit her so hard, her joints have got stiff, she starts crying for no good reason. And my old body, it's no use any more. It was an accident at work that did me in, but they only gave me this miserable little pension. It pays for my pills but not much more. And can you imagine it, they said I should be grateful to them for getting it, as I wasn't a registered worker? He was always telling me to put up my daily rate so I could save a bit for my old age, they depended on me, he used to say. He hated the mill owners, did you know that? And he was right about them depending on me. Here in the vast world of the entire valley, who did they always turn to when they wanted cauldrons soldered or their vats and pumps repaired? Always me. They'd call on me day and night, any time. I'd go to Aparecida or on the other side of the river to Caçapava in Jacareí. Back then it was all dairy farms here, pasture, big fields. Then it all went belly up. He saw this coming, he didn't prattle on, he didn't say much, but he knew before anyone else that all this farming was going to end. In its place came the factories, the parts manufacturers. One day we're all going to have to eat screws, there's not going to be any more milk or curd cheese or whey or butter or sugar, nothing. You think I'm exaggerating? Perhaps: he didn't say that, it's me speculating, he never said anything he hadn't thought through. See that pile of books in the garage? All his … and now they're going to waste. I went to school, learnt how to read and write, but after the accident this eye's been no use for reading, only for the sports page and then only a bit. Books were everything for him, nobody else could touch his books. He got the hang of reading very young. When he was a toddler, the other kids played around, he just wanted to read. Just think of that, sir. The others went off to fly kites, but he'd go and find a book in his uncle's house. I've told you about this uncle, haven't I? Rubens is my brother-in-law, my wife's brother, he ran the trade union; he was the one who gave my son this love of reading and this obsession with politics; but I'm not blaming Rubens, I don't blame anyone. It was fate. We're here to pay for our sins, aren't we? I remember my son at secondary school, coming up with this idea of producing a newspaper for students; it caused a right commotion. At prize-giving he gave the address; he was just 14 and already

speaking in public; it was at college that he got involved with the Catholic Church, the Paulo Freire movement I think they called it, they went to the poor parts of town and taught workers to read. When Jânio[1] resigned and had that fight with the military, he was glued to the radio. From then on, politics was his life. He only calmed down when he went to university, but nowadays I don't think that was for real, he just didn't want people to know what he was up to. Rubens had warned him, when they put the regiment at Caçapava on alert, well before all this happened, that they had to be very careful, both of them. He loved the pictures too, he went at lot, twice a week, as soon as they changed the film, he went. But football left him cold, he never went to a game, knew nothing about it, didn't know the names of the players. And he wasn't interested in girls, until that day he arrived with

1 This is a reference to Jânio Quadros, the Brazilian President who resigned abruptly for no apparent reason in August 1961 after only eight months in office, sparking off a political crisis that ultimately led to the 1964 military coup.

your daughter, just remembering it still gives me a turn. She came and he introduced her, a bit embarrassed he was, and her so courteous, so kind, even the neighbours loved her, she made us all happy. They'd go for walks in the town, have an ice-cream in the square, go to church fetes, the celebration for São Gonçalo the miracle-maker, the celebration for São João. It was not just him, the whole family took her to their heart. I'm telling the truth, that's what I feel. If it's too much for you, sir, I'll stop. When that advert came out in the newspaper, that photo of her as a 'disappeared', my daughter came and showed it to me, such a shock, I had to help the missus sit down. From then there's only been trouble, even the neighbours have behaved differently, glancing at us suspiciously, with mistrust, here everyone knows everyone else, news gets around in an instant, my daughter almost lost her job in the council; little by little it calmed down, but still today people cross the road to avoid us, but there's nothing we can do about it, is there? People are as they are. The missus liked her a lot, they loved chatting together, her and my daughter, the three of them, the real truth is that everyone took to her ... I can stop, if you like? ... they chatted about everything, even about me, about the aspirin I take three times a day, your daughter told me that I shouldn't take it if I wasn't in pain, she understood, with the exams she'd passed, but I know more about aspirins. She was like him, always had her nose in a book. Now I don't know what's going to happen to us. He was the rock in our family, he helped us out, he always knew what to do, he made sure we didn't lack anything. Now we've been left to cope on our own, it's not right, it's children that bury their parents, not parents that bury their children. The worst thing is, we can't even do that, we can't even bury his body.

Immunity, a paradox

A father looking for his disappeared daughter isn't afraid of anything. If he begins cautiously, it isn't because he is afraid, but because he's bewildered, like a blind man groping his way through a maze. The beginning is an apprenticeship, he needs to assess how dangerous it is, not for himself, because he isn't afraid of anything, but for others: friends, neighbours, university colleagues.

And at the outset there is hope, the unthinkable is ruled out; if you act with discretion you can pull it off. That's how organisations with vast experience of dealing with despots do it, low-key, no accusations. If only for this reason, the father looking for his disappeared daughter acts cautiously at first.

After many days have gone by and he's got nowhere, the father raises his voice; in anguish, he doesn't whisper any more, he approaches friends, friends of friends, even strangers; in this way he starts, still like a blind man with a stick, to map out the vastness of the wall of silence that will prevent him finding out the truth.

He discovers the wall without discovering his daughter. Soon he will tire of begging for attention. When the days become weeks and there's still no news, the father cries out, all control gone; he becomes irritating, annoying, with his tragic story, his impossible demand for justice.

The vortex goes on sucking people in, the repression is as brutal as ever, but the father who seeks his daughter fears it less and less. Broken-hearted but unflinching, he becomes aware of the paradox of his immunity. Everyone but him can be dragged into it, can be run over, or dumped by the side of the road. But the repression can't touch him, even when he says the unsayable. To touch him would be to confess, to admit guilt.

And he knows they can't touch him. He goes to the press, he demonstrates, waving a banner in the face of the dictatorship and defying the police; he marches in the city centre, like the Argentine mothers in the Plaza de Mayo, the half-dead who scare the living; dedicated to a task that only he can perform. He is fearless. He sees some people glancing at him fearfully, out of the corner of their eyes, while others look at him with sympathy.

Glancing in a shop mirror along one of the city avenues, he sees an old man with other old people, holding an enlarged picture of his daughter as if it were a placard, and he realises with a start how much he has changed. He is no longer himself, the writer, the poet, the teacher of Yiddish, he is no longer an individual but has become a symbol, the icon of a disappeared political activist's father.

When the weeks become months, he gets tired and does less, but doesn't stop. The father seeking his disappeared daughter never stops. His hope dies but not his persistence. Now he wants to know what happened. Where? When exactly? He needs to know so he can work out his share of the blame. But they don't tell him anything.

Another year and the dictatorship finally begins to lose strength. That's what everyone thinks; but it's not the decline that precedes death, rather it's a metamorphosis, slow and measured. As obstinate as ever, the father looking for his disappeared daughter will still hold up her enlarged picture for all to see, but the sympathetic looks become fewer and fewer. Other banners will be raised, more convenient ones. The icon is no longer needed, it causes discomfort. The father of the disappeared daughter will insist, refusing to accept common sense.

A few years later and life returns to normal, a normality that for most people has never been disturbed. Old people die, babies are born. The father searching for his disappeared daughter stops searching, defeated by exhaustion and indifference. He no longer holds up the photograph. He is no longer an icon. He is no longer anything. He is the useless trunk of a dried-up tree.

Two reports

Report from agent Souza, 20 May 1972.

Meeting of the regional command of ALN/RJ.[1] Activists already identified took part: Clemêncio (or Clemens or Alcides), Márcio (or Cid), Álvaro (or Fernando or Mário), and Rodriguez, not identified before, as well as this agent. Pick-up point – Praça Saenz Peña with Márcio, my only contact after liquidation of Yuri. The aforementioned met in a new location or an old one not used by this agent before. Location: block of tenement flats at 663 Conde de Bonfim, first floor kitchenette, flat 2, at the end of the corridor, with a way out through the window at the back to an electricity transmission station owned by Luz; there is no caretaker and no need to take the lift. Front door reinforced with two wooden crossbars. Thick rope tied to the window to facilitate escape in case of a raid. Márcio had the keys. Ten minutes later the above-identified Álvaro arrived, with an unknown person introduced as Rodriguez. Identification: Rodriguez is of average height, thin, black hair and strong features, with a jutting jaw and thick eyebrows that meet in the middle, aged between 28 and 30. A few minutes later and the already-identified Clemêncio arrived. He acted as the leader as soon as he arrived, although, as already reported, he is only 19 years old. Three of the terrorists were armed with snub-nose revolvers: Álvaro, Clemêncio and Márcio. Me as well, following instructions. The unknown element Rodriguez was not armed: he must be part of the support network, not the advance guard. Those named above already knew that the recent captures were the result

---

1 Rio de Janeiro branch of Ação Libertadora Nacional, the main urban guerrilla movement that fought the military regime.

of infiltration. Clemêncio said he had a suspect and suggested that a commission of enquiry be set up under his leadership with the objective of eliminating the informer. He did not reveal the name of the suspect. Márcio said they must act very cautiously and had to uncover evidence. Clemêncio spoke of the risk of the movement collapsing: they had to carry out both the enquiry and the elimination quickly, to intimidate those with any thought of giving up the struggle. He said that the idea of finding the traitor had great appeal and the elimination could help to regroup the organisation around the new strategy of a permanent insurrectional movement with foci dispersed deep in the interior of the country and with tactical actions in the cities. Rodriguez didn't give his opinion. He was introduced as coming from Paraná, but he must be from São Paulo, because, as stated in an earlier report, there is nothing left in Paraná. He scarcely said anything. I felt he wasn't happy about my presence. The meeting ended without changes to the procedures, meeting arrangements or passwords. No other action was discussed nor another meeting arranged, so this is all I have to report.

This hiding place was new to him: it must be one of the last, perhaps the very last, he thought. The meeting was short and nervous, as he'd expected. He'd supported the proposal for the elimination of the infiltrator, as he'd been told to do. Then he'd claimed security concerns for leaving early. He wanted to write his report with the details still clear in his head. He turned the corner and randomly hailed a taxi. The centre please, he said. He got the taxi to stop two blocks away from the Barão de Mesquita[2] and walked the rest of the way. He typed the report directly without bothering with notes, to save time. While he was typing, he couldn't help remembering the anguished faces at the meeting. He knew this was a key moment: the first meeting of the regional command after all the people were captured and their leader liquidated, they needed urgently to find the informer. There was a real risk that he would be unmasked and eliminated. Before the meeting he'd spent the afternoon on edge, going through in his head his last contacts

2   A Rio de Janeiro army barracks where political prisoners were tortured and killed.

with the movement, one by one, to be sure he hadn't left himself vulnerable, raised suspicions. He'd decided to go to the meeting only when he was sure they didn't suspect him. And also found time to meditate for half an hour. But what was happening on the other side? His side? His boss might get him to prolong the operation so that they could uncover new people, like this Rodriguez, for instance. Or his boss might decide they didn't need any more information. They've already decided to wipe out the remnants of the organisation, he knows that very well, they're only waiting for the right moment, they're all fucked, it's only a matter of time. Permanent insurrectional movement, these people are mad, totally out of touch with reality, absolute madness. But me, what will happen to me when it's all over? When I'm no longer any use, I become disposable. And I know too much. What guarantee have I got that they won't wipe me out too? Haven't they already done away with the bloke who infiltrated the VPR?[3]

Shit, what a mess I'm in. There has to be a way out. And to think I got into this mess because of women, all those women who used to go to the assemblies, and that damned Laura whose face I can still see, all covered in blood. A bank raid, when they started talking about that, that was when I should have got out. Expropriation, she said, and me, what's this got to do with me, was I ever asked? They offered me a way out to Algeria, they really wanted me to go. They were afraid I'd talk: it was that or going completely underground, that's what they said. I should have left the movement then, I'd have got away with it easily, I could have melted away and that would have been the end of it. But how could I have known it would end up in this nightmare?

He looked around, he was still alone, in the 'kennel'. The bastard calls us dogs. He thought back to that terrible night

<hr>

3   Vanguarda Popular Revolucionária, another guerrilla movement, founded in 1968.

when they'd pulled out one of his nails, told him they were going to pull them out one by one, it was then that he'd agreed to change sides. But now they didn't need him any more, what guarantee did he have? None. But he wasn't going to let them kill him after all he'd been through. He needed time to think of a way out. He pulled his report out of the typewriter, screwed it up into a ball and put it in his mouth. Just as well the sheets of paper he'd been given were flimsy and small. He waited until the ball had got wet and then began discreetly to chew it. He put another piece of paper in the typewriter and began another report:

Report from agent Souza, 20 May 1972.
Meeting of the command of ALN/RJ. Pick-up point in Praça Saenz Peña with Márcio, my only contact after liquidation of Yuri. Waited the prescribed 10 minutes without the contact appearing; returned 15 minutes later, as laid down in the norms, without the appearance of the agent. Operation aborted. Await instructions.

He was taking the report from the typewriter when the door opened and his boss appeared. He gulped down the paper ball and handed over the report, while desperately wondering how he could explain away his red face and the sweat running down his forehead.

A nightmare

That night K slept deeply for the first time since the disappearance of his daughter. The trip to the Baixada Fluminense[1] had left him exhausted. He woke up refreshed but disturbed by a dream he'd had, almost a nightmare. He'd felt as if he was being punished for his stupidity on the previous day. Dreams are always confused but this one more than usual, with strange scenes he was now trying to decipher. One came back forcefully to his mind. He was digging the ground with a shovel, it was an ordinary shovel, with a flat blade, yet each time he brought it up, it held a vast amount of earth, as if it were a mechanical digger, so the hole soon became very deep. There was an obvious interpretation for the dream: he should have dug a hole on the previous day and he hadn't, despite all the effort he'd made to find that forsaken spot in the Baixada Fluminense. He remembered that mulatto girl, with a baby on her lap, who'd pointed out the scrap-metal yard, the only one near the station. He'd reached the cave by taking four hundred paces towards the hills from the gate. And there he'd found the path and at the end of it the round granite rock, just as the journalist had said, the same journalist who'd told him that disappeared political prisoners had been buried there. But K

1   Lowlands in the state of Rio de Janeiro.

85

had looked at the hard, stony ground with its few dirty tufts of grass and weeds. No sign that the earth had been dug up. Perhaps it was then that the feeling of despair had begun to hit him. He'd also realised he'd made a mistake in not getting someone to come with him. While seeking help from so many important people, at home and abroad, he'd got cut off from the joint actions the families took, although it was clear – obviously – that all the families also carried out their own searches, mobilising people they knew, relatives by marriage, even distant ones, or work colleagues; they all did this and they had to. But some things shouldn't be done alone.

When he reached the spot, K also realised just how ridiculous the journalist's suggestion had been to hire a tractor in the town and get the driver to dig up the area. As if it was a simple business, digging up a skeleton or perhaps more than one, clumsily, so everything would be damaged, without an official body witnessing what was going on and drawing up a report, without any experts there, without involving the Brazilian Bar Association. That wasn't the right way to do it. It was as if he'd never really thought he'd actually dig up the spot. After so much false information, so many useless leads, perhaps he'd got hooked on the hunt, just for its own sake, so that he would have something to do. The worst moments were when he was alone, without anything to do. Then the image of his daughter was so strong it physically hurt him. That was why at the slightest hint of a lead, even if it didn't really add up, he leapt into action. That wasn't the case with this journalist; he was a serious person, with good police sources, famous for his investigative reporting. His instructions on how to get to the place had been completely accurate. But the spot could have been used to bury common criminals in the past, and not had anything to do with the political disappeared. And if he by himself had suddenly decided to get a tractor to dig up the ground he'd have certainly attracted attention. It was a dangerous thing to do. But it hadn't been fear that had stopped him. A father in search of his disappeared daughter isn't afraid of anything; after all he's been through, it doesn't matter what happens to him. No, it wasn't fear, it was despair, the sapping of his will, exhausted just by the effort of getting there and examining the spot. And the fact that he was alone, of course. He ought to have passed on the information to the Commission of the Families of the Disappeared, and together they could have decided what action to take. He could still do that, it would give meaning to the trip he'd done alone, he could present it as an initial checking of the information. This thought calmed him down.

Straightaway he remembered another part of the dream: he was at the bottom of the hole, still digging, and when he glanced up he saw faces around the hole looking down at him. It seemed as if he was already at the bottom of a grave, with everyone peering down, all his old literary friends, the Cohen brothers, Rosa Palatinik, the lawyer Lipiner, the Portuguese owner of the bakery, his Spanish neighbour, his partner in the shop, all familiar faces, yes familiar, like one big family, families of the disappeared. What had been the matter with him? Why hadn't he shared the information at their last meeting? All those faces of the families looking down at him. Thinking back, he couldn't remember how they looked. Were they angry? Or curious? Or indifferent? Or anxious? As for him, he went on digging, digging. Suddenly K remembered another scene in the dream, when his shovel had hit a stone and a snake had come out from under it and he'd killed it with a single blow before it could attack him. He'd jumped out of the hole in an instant and, though he hadn't been bitten by the snake, he was shivering as if he had a fever.

By then everyone else had gone, only the mulatto girl with the baby was still there, and this girl was now the very young maid – she must have been 14 or 15 years old – he'd employed long ago to look after his daughter when his wife had been taken ill, without energy for anything, after hearing the news about the war in Poland. His daughter had been only 3, and this girl, called Diva, had looked after her. In the dream he'd felt his shivering get worse when he looked at the child, it was his little daughter, and Diva was saying to him, come and lie down, it's time to take your quinine.

He remembered the malaria he'd caught when he'd been digging a piece of land in Água Fria, a piece of land he'd bought from a friend he'd trusted; and when he'd got there he'd found it was very boggy. He'd gone there to fence it, to mark it out, he'd had a shovel with a flat blade, and he'd killed three snakes there, and the land was soft, because it was a swamp, so bad that he'd caught that dratted malaria. He was only 38 at the time, it was the first piece of land he'd managed to buy; and afterwards, when it had increased in value, despite being boggy, he'd sold it and used the money to make the down payment on their house. It was at that time, with his daughter still a toddler, his wife traumatised, and him delirious with malaria, that the young mulatto girl, Diva, had looked after his daughter. He'd forgotten about Diva. What had happened to her? Diva had also disappeared. One day she'd handed in her notice and left, after living with them for over a decade. Although she always ate on her own, she'd been like a member of the family: she'd slept in his daughter's bedroom, they'd been almost like sisters. She'd left without saying where she was going, without leaving an address, as if she were angry about something.

But, of course, she just disappeared, no one disappeared her; she must have got tired of being a maid, found a husband, and moved out of the neighbourhood, the city, but the way she left had upset his daughter, the whole family had been shaken by it. In the dream she returns with a child on her lap, and K stretches out both his hands to pick up the child. He doesn't know how to do it, he hasn't had much practice, but he stretches out his hands, puts them underneath her and lifts her up into his arms; and the child is smiling, she's a toddler, but she has his daughter's face.

Passion

I

At first it was fear. A lot of fear. Fear that he would harm my brother, my family; fear that he would harm me. Today it's passion, I'm telling you, pure passion, mad passion. On both sides, mine and his. And you can't judge passion, passion happens. You haven't come here to judge me, have you?

Sometimes I think it was the rain. I arrived soaked through, my thin blouse sticking to my body, water running down from my hair, my trousers dripping, and me there, defenceless, shivering with cold, like a small bird paralysed with fear as a snake draws closer. He could have done anything to me, attacked me, raped me, anything. Later he told me he'd got a real hard-on that day. I know you're a woman who doesn't use language like this, but that's the way I am. I'm sorry.

So what did he do? That day he didn't do anything. He sent for a towel. He waited until I'd dried myself. He gave me time to collect my thoughts. He even offered me brandy, to warm me up, he said, a real gentleman. It was on the following day that it happened, when I came back with the two photos of Zinho he said he needed for the passport. He put the photos on a table and took me into another room, a kind of annexe, with a bed and a toilet, and without saying anything he lifted up my dress, pulled down my knickers and pulled me towards him. I gave myself to him.

Was that what I wanted? I think so. At least, it's what I expected. I'd even prepared for it. I went to the hairdresser, I put on a low-cut dress, a loose one. I'd noticed the way he'd looked at me that first day. And would it have made any difference if I'd fought him off? None at all. Once you step into that building, there's no way back. He's such a powerful man, such a big shot. No woman could have stood up to him. And I wouldn't have got the passport, would I?

But what matters now is that it turned into passion. And then it doesn't matter whether he's a criminal, whether he's married or single. Nothing. I don't know if you've experienced a passion like this, have you? If you try to repress it, it only grows, it becomes an illness, it completely takes you over. You mustn't think that love and passion are the same thing. Passion is madness, it's blindness, you can't tell right from wrong any more. It's as if he hypnotised me. Because, if you think about it, how can I be living with a man everyone says is a monster?

II

I know what they say about him. You needn't tell me. What do you think I went to see him for? I went there for the same reason as you came here today. To ask a favour. To implore him to help me. I knew he was the only person who could save my brother. I'd done everything I could, you know. I'm a lawyer. I know influential people. But there was nothing I could do. Zinho was abroad and in a lot of trouble. The only way out for him was to flee the place, but he couldn't get to the Brazilian embassy. He thought about trying to get a safe-conduct from another country and then leaving. But if he did that and was caught, he could be found dead the next day, or disappear no one knows how.

He was the only one who could sort it out. I heard this from an important person, a lawyer I worked with, until he went to the Supreme Court and stopped working in this business. By 'worked with him', I mean I discovered small farmers who hadn't registered their land properly or who needed money urgently and then he bought their land at knockdown prices. It was this man who gave me the boss's telephone. Can you believe it? He answered it on the first ring. It's the number I'm still using today. A kind of hot line. The only people who have the number are me and a few powerful people.

I call him boss and he calls me sweetheart. He called me sweetheart for the first time when he handed me the passport. He said: here it is, sweetheart, make sure your brother gets it and we won't talk about it any more. Sometimes, when we're having sex, he calls me his babe. In bed, that's fine. But at other times it's only sweetheart. I'd feel bad if he called me his babe publicly. You understand, don't you? I'm an independent woman, I have a profession. But sweetheart is fine. It's affectionate.

III

We have a deal. He doesn't ask what I'm doing and I don't ask what he's doing. It's not that I don't ask him anything. It's more complicated than that, as it always is between a man and a woman, isn't it? One morning I mentioned a name, just said it as if I didn't want anything, as if I was reading the newspaper, and then waited to see how he'd react. He knew I did it on purpose. He's very sharp. But he pretended not to know what I was up to. After that first time, I've done it again a few times. It's a game he plays with me to please me. He'll do anything to please me. He tries to reply without showing he's replying.

And I don't push him too far. I've learnt how to understand what he means, even if he doesn't say things clearly. If he says 'sweetheart, forget that name', or something like that, then I know the worst has happened. He only reacted differently once. He said 'These newspapers don't know anything. This subversive is a long way away, using a different name.' He said it in such a way I felt sure he was the one who had let her go. He seemed to be proud of it.

Don't push me. Calm down. I'm getting there. I'm telling you what it's like, because it's complicated. It's a delicate matter, you have to try to understand how it works, just as I had to. So last Friday I mentioned your son's name casually, as if I was reading it in a paper. And do you know what happened? Just hearing the name, he tensed up. I was even afraid he was going to explode. But he looked at me seriously, his cup of coffee in the air, said nothing for a few seconds, as if he was trying to calm down or was thinking what to say – I'm telling you all this, in detail, so you can feel what I felt – and then he said, 'sweetheart, forget that name, don't mention it any more here or elsewhere'. And I understood. Do you understand? Your son's dead. He doesn't exist any more. I'm sorry but that's how it is. Your son's dead. Damn it!

IV

Drink some of this water. That's right. No, I don't have any children but I know what you're feeling, because Zinho is more like a son to me than a brother. That's why I risked everything to save him. I call him Zinho because he was my *nenezinho*, my little baby brother. There were five of us, I was the only girl. I was 12 when Zinho was born, a late baby. The rest of us were grown up or nearly grown up. My mother had post-natal depression, the baby almost died from neglect. I was the one who saved him. My brothers were all older than me and had gone their own way, set up businesses. I looked after Zinho as if he was my son. The only reason I didn't breastfeed him was because I hadn't yet got breasts! I was his mother, I've always been his true mother. But today he won't even talk to me, he rejects me as if I had leprosy. Him and the others. The only person who still talks to me is my mother. Mothers understand, they aren't like other people. My mother knows I was the one who saved Zinho from being killed, because he couldn't have escaped from where he was without a passport. My life changed completely because of him and today he rejects me.

V

So you're asking me if I knew beforehand that all this could happen? I had an inkling. I knew I was going down a dangerous path with no way back. But I didn't have time to think. On that rainy afternoon, when he answered the phone on the first ring, my heart was in my mouth. My lawyer friend had told me: ask him straight out, don't beat about the bush. So that's what I did. And he replied: 'Where are you at the moment?' 'I'm in a public phone box', I said, 'I've just left the gym'. And he said: 'Can you come here?' Do you understand? It was a test. I know because I'm a lawyer. I've done the same myself lots of times. You test the person, you see if they're really committed, ready to risk everything. I knew it was a test, that I had to plunge ahead or give up, that it was a make-or-break moment, but I didn't have time to think it through properly. So I said: 'I'm coming. Give me the address and I'll come.' Of course I knew the address. Everyone knows that building. It terrifies people just to catch a glimpse of it. But I wanted confirmation from him, to know I could arrive there and say: 'I've come to talk to so-and-so. He's expecting me.'

I know about that case of the priest who killed himself because of him. I don't know everything but what I do know makes me feel ill. I read about it in the newspaper. When I can, I read about him. After all, he's my man. We don't talk about these things; as I said, we have this pact, but I want to know. I need to know, to try to understand. How is it that a man who treats me so well can treat others so abominably? I'm no saint, I take advantage when I can, but the monstrous things they say he does, I tell you, they really frighten me … I feel panicky, just from reading about them.

Once he said: 'It's a war, and in a war you kill or are killed.' He thinks quite simply that priests shouldn't get involved in politics. I agree with him but I still have this kind of respect I had in Paraná, that a priest is a man of God. As a child I prayed a lot. And then Zinho was a delicate child, he was always ill, and I prayed for him to get better. I didn't have any one to turn to so I prayed.

Once he said that a priest who gets involved in politics isn't a priest, he's a terrorist. That's when I realised he hates priests. It's one thing not to like them, which is how I feel today. It's quite another thing to hate them. When he speaks of priests, the disgust shows on his face. Sometimes he gets angry and goes red in the face. Once he said: 'These priests are all perverts.' I've never asked him, but I've got the impression that some priest molested him when he was a altar boy. I know he was a altar boy because I've seen a picture of him as one.

He was delighted that day they arrested the Dominicans. It seems they took over a restaurant in Lapa so the whole team could celebrate. I've never seen him so happy, as if he'd got rid of a weight from his back. I knew about this get-together because they arranged it all on the phone and I listened. That night he arrived late and leapt on me like a wild animal. It's the only time I've felt really frightened, just as I did that first day. My heart was racing. I thought at one point he was going to strangle me, that he was torturing me, as if I was one of the priests. Can you imagine it? When I awoke the next morning, he'd already gone. I had a lot to think about that morning. But I had no one to talk to. Even my brothers had turned their backs on me. It was then that I realised just how isolated I'd become, without family or friends. I was seen as a monster just like him, a hated woman, whom the neighbours despised, as if I was the lowest of the low. Just me and him. I think that's why I agree to see people like you. I can't do anything to help. And it's not even because I feel sorry for you. It's because it makes me feel like a human being again, even if I have to tell you bad news.

VII

Is he a sadist? Not with me. Not even that night, when they arrested the Dominicans. He acted roughly, brutally even, but he wasn't a sadist. What he has is a real hatred of communists, hatred and scorn. I can see this in the way he talks on the phone. If they're dealing with communists, he thinks anything goes, he can crush them like cockroaches. He only feels a bit of respect for them if they fight back. I think that's one of the reasons why he treated the priest so badly, because he didn't put up much resistance. Though I suppose, as he was a priest, he was going to be treated badly whatever he'd done.

He hates priests more than he hates communists. Can you believe that? The hatred he felt for that priest was personal, he hated him as a person. The hatred he feels for communists is different, they brainwashed him with this idea that he has to wipe them out at any cost. That's how I see it. In a way the military blackmailed him into it, saying they'd forget the other crimes he'd been charged with if he took on the communists.

Don't get me wrong: I'm not defending him or justifying what he does. Not at all. But do you think these communists were all saints? Well, you should know that there were informers in all their groups, not policemen who'd infiltrated them, but communists betraying communists. They were the dogs, he called them the dogs. I used to hear him saying on the phone: call in the dog. Or fix a meeting with the dog.

One day I was reading the paper and I mentioned a writer, a writer of children's stories, who'd been arrested. And he said: 'He's a fucking coward. I didn't even have to light my cigarette. I just said I'd bring in his son, and the bastard gave us the names of more than fifty people, people who were and people who weren't.' That was the only time he admitted torturing people. This talk of lighting a cigarette, bringing in the son. I hate that kind of thing. It was the only time he broke our agreement that he wouldn't talk at home about the things he did at work.

VIII

I have other flings and so does he. And we both accept that. We agreed to keep our affair secret. After all he's married. And I didn't want anyone to know. Especially Zinho. On the second day I asked him to keep it secret and he said he would. With all these bars and restaurants, with all the people coming and going in this street up to the early hours of the morning, it's easy to cover things up. And you saw what the entrance is like, didn't you? You just have to walk down a few steps and you're here. No foyer. No doorkeeper. He comes almost every night. He tells his wife, who suffers from ill health, that he's working. He doesn't come at a regular time and he always comes in an official car without a number plate. He gets out a block before this building or after it. It's not just because he wants to keep our affair secret. He's also concerned about security. He doesn't bother so much now that Marighella's dead.[1] Before that he was much more careful. He himself told me my phone was bugged. He said it was for security reasons. He also said he'd have a bodyguard. Someone comes a little while before he arrives, and then again a little while before he leaves. He stands on the other side of the road. He always phones before he leaves.

We arranged for him never to answer the phone. I'd be the one to do that and, if it was for him, I'd hand the phone over. There was a password. In the beginning it was 'I want to speak to the boss' and then it changed to 'I want to speak to my manager.' Only a few people had the number, and they only used it in an emergency. But once there was that international call. 'Can I speak to the police officer, please? It's urgent.' I handed him the phone. The person hadn't used the password but he'd said it was urgent and it was international so I thought I'd better. But it was trap set by the communists. They'd heard a rumour of what was going on and they wanted to confirm it. It was after this that Zinho broke off relations with me. And then the rest of the family. And then the few friends I had left, but for me the most painful thing is Zinho's rejection. I think he was behind the call; he wanted proof. Now we're not so careful. He answers the phone as often as I do. But he's also increased security again.

IX

I know you're not interested in my story. No need to look embarrassed. And you needn't thank me. It's just painful for me to give you bad news. But deep down you knew, didn't you? They all do but they hope against hope that they're wrong. Or they're perhaps feeling guilty, feel they must go on searching,

1   Carlos Marighella was the founder and leader of the Aliança Libertadora Nacional (ALN), the main urban guerrilla organization that fought the military dictatorship.

must go on deceiving themselves, keeping busy. As I said, you're not the first person to have come to talk to me. And I know it's a big step for you. Let's be clear: coming to talk to a person like me, the mistress of that monster, isn't like going to talk to a well-known general, who defends what's going on but has never dirtied his hands, or to a government supporter, or even to a jailer, who's only obeying orders. Coming to talk to a person like me shows you're prepared to do anything. I know what's what, I know you all think of me as beyond the pale. You'll say to yourself afterwards: I even went to talk to that dreadful woman. It's not so very different from what I did to save Zinho. Didn't I go in a loose dress that showed off my breasts? Wasn't that how it all began? And now I need you, to make me feel I'm still useful, despite the mess I'm in. So that's why you don't need to thank me. I should be thanking you.

X

Of course it wasn't my fault I fell in love. Is falling in love ever anyone's fault? Now we're beginning to understand each other. We've already talked as a mother to another mother, and now we're talking woman to woman. It's only a woman's fault if she doesn't give in to her passion. The crime isn't falling in love but repressing it. Then it's a crime against herself. That's true for women and men too, don't you think? I'm going to tell you something very personal, very private. Sometimes, when we're having sex, for a fraction of a second I put myself in the place of another woman, and this woman is a prisoner who is being gang-raped. I've never told anyone this, not even a priest during confession.

In fact, I stopped going to confession some time ago. As I said before, as a child I was very religious, my father as well, bless his soul. But studying Law changes people a lot. I lost all trust in priests. I even understand now why he's so scornful of them. But, do you know, one day, after I'd started living with him, I went to confession. When I knew I was in love with him and him with me, I panicked. I went and told the priest all about it, about the man I was living with, and all the dreadful things they said about him. And do you know what the priest said? That to have a sexual relationship outside marriage was a sin, but that God would forgive me. So for him this was the sin? And the rest? The deaths, the tortures, aren't they sins? To sleep with a man who did all this: wasn't that to live in a state of sin? I went back a second time, and this time the priest said that all that was happening to me was part of God's plan. It was then I decided to stop going to confession.

XI

Of course I've thought of leaving him. At one time, I used to think about it every day. It wasn't that the passion had ended. It hasn't even now. It's the price I'm paying for it. But how could I leave him? And what would the consequences be? That first day I was really frightened. I was frightened of a cruel and unscrupulous man, who has power of life and death over people, people like Zinho. I've still got that fear, but there's a new one too: fear of what a jealous man, a man who's beside himself with anger for being abandoned, might do. How many men have killed their wives in this situation, even when she hasn't gone off with someone else? And he might well react like that. Nowadays I don't think so much about leaving him. What would I gain from it? I'm so isolated. My brothers reject me. I can't see my nephews and nieces. I feel as if I've been branded on the forehead, just like they brand cattle on their hindquarters in Paraná. And it's never going to end. Just as you're going to live with the pain of losing your son until the day you die, so I'm going to bear this brand. My only consolation is that I saved Zinho. You couldn't manage to save your son. That's sad, so sad, and it needn't have been like that. Let me see you out. No, let me say it again. You mustn't thank me. It's me who thanks you.

Memories, an inventory

The photos were in a mess, mixed up with letters, negatives and a pile of medical prescriptions. K found the blue box by chance, behind two volumes of his Yiddish encyclopaedia, which had bindings of the same colour. It was as if his daughter had hidden it there for no one to find. Or had she put it there on purpose so that he'd be the one to find it?

When he started looking at the pictures, he became aware once again of how little he'd known about her life and how much he still didn't know. Along with the expected pictures – her with two close friends whom he knew well, her at work in a white lab coat – there were others that took him by surprise.

In one of them his daughter is riding a horse. Where was she when this picture was taken? In another she's whirling around, dancing with others. K lifts out the photos one by one and looks at them slowly, precious relics of his daughter's life. Looking at her by a bandstand in a small square, he tries but fails to work out which town she was visiting when this picture was taken.

And it's only now, seeing her frozen in time and space, that he realises just how fragile a person she'd been. K had never imagined that photos could provoke such strong feelings.

Some of them even seemed to want to tell a story. Until then only the words of a Pushkin or a Sholem Aleichem had had such an effect on him. He'd thought photos were only a way of recording an episode, proving that something had happened, or of providing a portrait needed for a document. But these photos of his daughter radiated delicacy and sensitivity. They seemed to capture his daughter's soul. He felt something of her presence in them, almost as if her ghost hovered over them. They made him shiver.

There weren't many photos, and only one of her as a child, sitting next to the younger of her two brothers, in a child's pushchair. She must have been 5 or 6, her brother 10 or 11, far too big for the pushchair. They seemed to be enjoying themselves. Were they in a playground? Or in the Jardim da Luz park?

Now he remembers. It was in Jardim da Luz. He'd taken them out for the afternoon. Soon after that her brother had pushed her into the lake when she was bending over to look at the carp. That kind of rough fun, which had left her feeling humiliated, was typical of the two of them. They had bought the picture from a street photographer, who had been working in the park. K had never learnt how to use a camera.

There were also copies of the two photos he already had – one of her at her graduation, looking solemn, proud of herself but restrained, looking away from the camera, which emphasised her sharp profile and her serious look, and the other of her sitting on the edge of a bed or sofa, her face thinner than ever, her thin lips sucked in and a look of great anguish on her face. He realises with a start that they don't seem like pictures of the same person.

He'd taken these two photos to the police when he'd registered her disappearance, and then later to that so-called doctor in Rio de Janeiro. For obscure reasons, perhaps because he felt guilty – although it's difficult to imagine a man like that, who is like an animal with no sense of right or wrong, feeling guilt – this doctor was willing to identify disappeared political prisoners he'd seen being tortured. His role in those sessions had been to prevent the people being tortured from dying before they'd revealed the information the executioners wanted. K had also taken the only photo of his son-in-law that he'd managed to get hold of from his family. It was only now, rummaging through the blue box, that he found one of them together.

K relived that meeting with the doctor, the profound dislike he'd felt for him and had been unable to conceal properly when he walked into the room. When shown the graduation picture, the doctor had been emphatic. He didn't recognise her. When shown the second picture of her, the one with her suffering face, he'd repeated the denial but K sensed more hesitation in him. Then, when he saw the photo of her husband, another denial, but this time K was sure that something had upset the man. So K showed the pictures again, but the doctor repeated his denial. K returned to São Paulo feeling frustrated and unhappy, mainly because he was sure the doctor knew something he didn't want to say. It must be something terrible. And it was his fault that he hadn't managed to get it out of him.

As he goes through the pictures and examines them slowly, one by one, trying to work out from the hairstyle or the clothes when and where each of the snapshots was taken, K feels more and more depressed. He can't find any photos of her with him or her mother or elder brother. It was as if she had no father or mother, and only one brother.

It's true that she scarcely knew her elder brother. When she was born, he'd already rebelled against the family and was living more in the street than at home. She must have been about 9 years old when he left Brazil to live in a kibbutz in Israel.

He knew why there were no pictures of her mother: by then she had lost all joy in life. His daughter had been born during the war, when her mother was already disturbed by the rumours about her family in Poland. And when she was growing up, it grew worse, since the confirmation of their extermination left her mother permanently depressed.

K is upset at not finding any photos of him with his daughter, even though she'd been his favourite child and he'd taken her to school every day, spoiling her like a princess. He realised he'd never put any photos in an album. Every family had an album of photos of their children, except his.

His wife had made an album of the elder son, her first-born, with pictures of him from when he was a baby to his wedding, then of him very thin in the kibbutz, and then of the granddaughters. There were pictures of the younger son, the almost obligatory pictures of a child smiling on various occasions. They had put them in pretty frames but they hadn't made an album. But of the daughter, nothing. Neither an album nor framed pictures. Her mother had considered her ugly. K knew this. That must have been the reason, he thought. But he hadn't thought of his daughter as ugly; even so he hadn't made an album.

K had brought from Europe an album of those blurred sepia pictures that possess a certain magic. Portraits of his parents, and of uncle Beni, before he went off to fight with the Red Army, of his brothers in Berlin, of the old house they lived in in Wloclawek. And photos of his literary friends, the whole group together, in Warsaw. He was there too, a young lad in the middle of that group of important people. He was especially proud of the picture of him beside the great writer Joseph Opatoshu. He recalled that his wife had filled the last two empty pages of this album with two or three pictures of her sons, and a photo of her first granddaughter. But no picture of her daughter.

K was struck by a series of photos taken, according to the writing on the back of some of them, in Paraty in 1966. Although he could also see in these pictures his daughter's delicate fragility, she seemed a mature woman at ease with herself, with the calm expression of a person who is going through a good phase of life. Her hair, tied back, framed her face discreetly. She looked elegant in all these pictures.

That was eight years before the tragedy. K tried to work out which was the last to be taken in that handful of snapshots. He went back to the one with the sad face, which he'd shown to the police and the doctor. He discovered another four from the same sequence, also taken on the bed or sofa. The same light flowery blouse, the same depressed face, the same tight look of helplessness. He was sure she was already fearing the worst.

K places the lid on the box and puts it back where he found it. He thinks: if I'd taken a photo album to Rio, showing her whole life from her birth to the eve of her disappearance, perhaps he would have recognised her and explained what had happened. But K didn't have a photo album. He'd never even thought of making one, so busy he'd been with literature and newspaper articles.

Therapy

Her face is well-proportioned but inexpressive, her lips thin and her eyes small and lifeless; her clothes are unremarkable, grey blouse and skirt, like a work uniform. Her thick black hair is cut short. She is short and stocky. Hesitantly, she goes into the psychologist's room, wringing her hands and looking down. The therapist consults a file and invites her to sit down.

'Jesuína Gonzaga, you're 22 years old and you say you can't sleep and have hallucinations. So you want a doctor's certificate so you can get time off work for treatment. Is that right?'

'I came here because my boss told me to. It must be written on that piece of paper that my firm says that my nerves are bad and I can't work properly.'

'Yes, that's what the doctor at Ultragás says. What's your work there, Jesuína?'

'I'm a cleaner. Before, I helped in the kitchen, but they shouted at me a lot and I asked to be moved, I said I'd rather be a cleaner. But even now any little thing gets on my nerves and I start trembling. I feel faint and have to sit down. I also get upset if there's too much dirt.'

'They must like you a lot not to have sacked you, Jesuína,

don't you think? Tell me something. When they took you on, did they send you for a medical examination?'

'I didn't have any medical tests. And that's right, they say they're not going to sack me, they say I shouldn't worry. They have this idea of me getting a letter from the doctor saying I'm too ill to work, and then perhaps me being certified as disabled so that I don't ever have to work again. But the first step, they say, is to get a doctor's letter. I don't like them there. They keep themselves to themselves. Have a lot of secrets. But they're good to me. Perhaps it's because someone high up got me the job.'

The therapist looks at the file again. It often happens, when it's for rough work, like cleaning, that they don't send off new employees for the medical check-up they're supposed to have. Or they contract the work out and then they don't have to bother with any of that. But she says it was someone high up who got her the job.... Could she have had an affair with one of the directors, even though she's not pretty? Or perhaps something else? Could she be the illegitimate daughter of one of them? The therapist's getting curious and decides to encourage her to talk.

'And what do you want? To be certified as disabled?'

'Who wouldn't want to be paid without having to work? But what I really want is to get better. To be like other people. I get a lot of noise in my head. I try to get rid of it but I can't. I'd like to get a proper boyfriend, enjoy myself, but my workmates don't ask me out any more, they say I'm a pain, that I'm always depressed.'

The therapist's starting to feel sorry for her. She has a daughter of the same age.

'Are you getting any treatment for this?'

'I've been on sleeping pills, the company's doctor gave me a prescription. It's a pill that needs a prescription but it's not working as well as it did in the beginning.'

The young woman hesitates for a few seconds and then starts speaking again in a stronger voice:

'There's something I haven't told you because it's a bit embarrassing. I often bleed when I shouldn't, you know, just like those days in the month, and sometimes it shows.... It just takes my boss to get angry with me or someone to raise their voice and I start bleeding. That's why the others can't stand me. Before I joined the firm, I used to bleed at odd times, but it's got worse. Before it was only when I was really frightened, when I was terrified. Now anything starts it off. I have started to take precautions all the time, just like those days in the month.'

The therapist asks casually, pretending to read the file:

'Jesuína, who is this high-up person who got you the job?'

The young woman lowers her eyes and doesn't reply. The therapist repeats the question, now looking at the young woman, who still doesn't say anything.

'Jesuína, I'm a doctor here. I'm not your boss and I don't have anything to do with your firm. This is the public health service, nothing to do with your company. I won't say anything to anyone. But I can only help you if you're honest with me.'

The young woman remains silent, her shoulders a little more sunken, still looking at the floor.

'Jesuína, if they're talking about you getting a disability allowance, it's because they think you're really ill. As you yourself said, you're only 22 years old. We need to get you better. I know some things are difficult to talk about, but you must make an effort.... Jesuína, what's this noise in your head that you want to get rid of? What is it?'

Jesuína still refuses to speak. The therapist is starting to get irritated and, making an effort not to raise her voice, she says:

'And another thing. This is the public health service. That doesn't mean I'm going to treat you any worse than I'd treat a private patient, but there's a long queue of people outside waiting to be seen. If you don't want to be open with me, I don't really want to do this, but I'll have to move on. I'll give you a prescription for sleeping pills and an anti-depressant, and tell you to come back in six months. Job done.... Is that what you really want?'

Jesuína shakes her head but still doesn't answer.

'Jesuína, is that what you want?'

Finally the young woman speaks, but her voice is weak, she can scarcely be heard, and she has to make an effort to get the words out.

'The person who got the job for me was the police officer, Delegate Fleury.'

'Fleury from the death squad? Is that who you're talking about, Jesuína? Sérgio Paranhos Fleury?'

The therapist, amazed, begins to stand up but stops herself so as not to alarm the young woman. She leans back in her chair, moving slowly. She's afraid she's getting involved in something dangerous. But her curiosity wins out. Can the young woman really be telling the truth?

'Yes. That's him. I did some work for him. Once that was over and the house was closed down, he got me this job. He was a very close friend of Dr Alberto, who used to be the owner of the firm where I work. He was killed by terrorists, but Dr Fleury spoke to the people who took over and they gave me a job.'

The therapist tries to hide her fear and to make it appear that she's merely seeking clarification.

'You say you did some work for Fleury. But I don't understand what you're saying. Do you mean the hallucinations have something to do with this?'

The young woman takes a deep breath, finally ready, it seems, to make a clean breast of it. She speaks clearly, though still in fits and starts.

'It's complicated. I'll have to begin at the beginning. Dr Fleury got me out of Taubaté prison and took me to that house. I was on conditional release and he took me there to work for him. I stayed at the top of the house, making coffee, preparing sandwiches, taking water to the inmates and cleaning.'

Jesuína hesitates and adds: 'Every time he visited, he also had sex with me.'

'So is that why you've hallucinations and bleeding? He was raping you?'

'No, that wasn't a problem. I did it because I did it. I even liked it. The hallucinations started later, after the house was closed down.'

'House. What kind of house was this, Jesuína? From the way you're speaking it sounds like a brothel. I hope you don't mind me using the word.'

'No, nothing like that. You haven't understood. It was a prison that looked like a house. Sometimes he told me to listen to what one of the prisoners – it could be a man or a woman – was saying. I cleaned their cells, I took them water. He told me to be nice to them, see if I could get them to give me a message or a phone number. I had to pretend I felt sorry for them, offer to tell their families what had happened to them, that sort of thing. Sometimes they believed me and gave me a message written on a scrap of paper. I would hand it over straightaway to Dr Fleury. I pretended I was a prisoner there too, that I was forced to do the cleaning. I was told to tell them that I'd killed my stepfather because he'd raped me and that I'd been sent from Bangu to work in the house. That was the story I had to tell them, but only bit by bit, to win over their confidence. Once they put me in a cell with a woman prisoner. But that only happened once.'

'And this story of killing your stepfather, Jesuína. Is it true or did you make it up?'

'It's a lie. He didn't die and I didn't really hurt him. I tried but I only had a tiny knife. I was only 13 years old. He raped me for the first time when I was 12. He waited for my mother to go off to work and then he raped me. It's something I'll never forget. He was like an animal. I lost a lot of blood. When I saw all that blood on the bed, I thought I was dying. That's when the bleeding began, because of my stepfather. Every time he came near me, even before he seized hold of me, I started bleeding. Then I ran away and got involved in drugs. A man helped me. I've never been back home. I went to prison because of the drugs, not because of my stepfather. The man who helped me sold drugs and I ended up getting hooked.'

'The prisoners you had to win over, did they believe your story?'

'There wasn't really time for them to believe me or not. They were only in the house for a day or two. Dr Fleury said I should keep it simple. If they asked, I should stick to the story of my stepfather. Dr Fleury used to arrive with the prisoners, or soon after. He came from São Paulo, that was it, and he would question them that night or the following morning, and then the prisoners disappeared. A few days later some more would arrive.'

Horrified by what she's heard, the therapist feels her hands shaking. She tries to take notes, but she can't. She takes a sip of water, serving herself from a jug on a table near her desk, and offers Jesuína a glass, which she accepts. She needs to think. She's terrified by what she's heard, but at the same time she wants to know more. The faces of old colleagues and friends race through her mind. She feels that Jesuína is concealing some dreadful secret. She asks, carefully:

'Have you received any treatment for this bleeding? Has anybody looked into it?'

'No, the treatment I got was to get me to stop using drugs. After Dr Fleury shut down the house, I was sent to a house in São Bernardo. A house run by priests. I stayed there for six months and I got better. Dr Fleury then arranged a job for me at the barracks in Quitaúna, but I soon got involved in drugs again. I went back to be treated and this time I think I was properly cured. I've been clean for three and a half years.'

The therapist waits for a few seconds and then asks:

'You've talked a lot about this house that Fleury closed down. Where was this house, Jesuína?'

The young woman doesn't say anything.

'Jesuína, you needn't say everything at once and you needn't say anything you don't want to. But, if you're going to get better, you have to face up to your past, you have to get rid of the things that are bothering you, that cause these hallucinations and prolong the bleeding. Was it something to do with the prisoners?'

Jesuína remains silent, her shoulders hunched.

'Jesuína, tell me something about this house, anything that comes into your head. Tell me whatever you remember. It's going to make you feel better.'

'It was an ordinary house, like the others in the street. It was big house, built on the side of a steep slope, a hill in Petrópolis. It was an ordinary road, with big houses belonging to rich people. The gardens were big too. The house had high walls around it. And there was some woodland on both sides. Nobody could see what was happening inside. When a car arrived, the garage door opened automatically, the car came in and the prisoner was straightaway taken to the bottom of the house, where the cells were. There were only two cells. I almost always stayed in the top part of the house, the part that gave on to the road. In the bottom part, as well as the cells, there was a closed-off area where they interrogated prisoners. But you could hear the screams throughout the house. I still hear them. There are a lot of screams in my nightmares. But lower still, in the back yard, almost at the bottom of the hill, there was something else, a kind of shed or garage. I sometimes had to clean the closed room where they questioned prisoners, but they never sent me to that other place in the back yard.'

The therapist asks gently:

'What happened there, Jesuína?'

But Jesuína ignores her and carries on:

'I looked after the prisoners, I cleaned the cells, I tried to get friendly with them. They were in a terrible state. Their eyes bulging. Trembling. Some of them spoke to themselves. Others seemed to be half-dead, they were in a kind of stupor.'

'You said that after a few days the prisoners disappeared. Where did they go?'

The young woman doesn't say anything.

'You were starting to tell me about this other place, right at the bottom of the yard.'

Jesuína seems to be in a world of her own, almost talking to herself:

'One day a lovely looking boy arrived. He was thin, delicate-looking but, poor lad, one of his legs was bleeding heavily, an enormous wound, it was doing him in. But, instead of treating it, they put salt in the wound…. He stayed in the cell for three days before they took him down to the yard…. I'll never forget him, so delicate, so handsome, his leg just one huge wound. This one I really tried to help, I wasn't putting it on, but he couldn't even talk….'

'Do you remember his name?'

'He was so delicate. He told me his name, his first name, Luiz. Just that. He wrote down a phone number on a piece of paper, I think it was his mother's, but I was so frightened and upset that I lost it. I didn't give it to Dr Fleury.'

'You were talking about the part downstairs … '

'Whenever a new prisoner arrived, Dr Leonardo, a doctor from Rio, would appear; when the prisoner was in a poor way during the questioning, he went into the closed room and carried out an examination. I knew that when Dr Leonardo left they'd finished with the prisoner, and would take him or her down to the yard.'

'Finished with the prisoner...' the therapist repeats the words and is just going to ask the young woman another question, when she starts speaking again:

'One day they brought in two older men, they must have been over 60, well dressed, in suits, they put each of them in a separate cell. They didn't beat them, but they soon took them out, first one and then the other, two hours later....'

The therapist asks:

'You said earlier that they once put you in a cell with a woman prisoner. Why did you mention that?'

'Because I can't forget her. She had one of those faces you never forget. They brought her to the house late, not during the night, but at the end of the afternoon, her arm was hurt, I think they'd twisted it, but her face was fine. I've got this thing about her face because of what happened next.'

'What happened next?'

They told me to go into her cell, without telling me what I was supposed to do there. I tried to talk to her. She told me her name and then didn't say anything else. She told me her full name, I think it was her full name, but I don't remember it because it was complicated. She said it out loud, kind of recited it, like someone who knows they're going to die and wants to leave their name so that people will know.'

'And then what happened?'

'Dr Fleury arrived, during the night. He took me out of the cell and asked me if the girl had said anything, so I said no, just her name and then she'd gone quiet.... He told them to put me back in her cell. The girl seemed like a statue, she was in the same place, silent, just as before.'

Suddenly, Jesuína stops talking.

'Jesuína, my dear. You were talking about this girl.'

117

'Dr Fleury sent me back in with her, to see if she'd say anything more. In the early hours of the morning, I heard someone arrive and go into the room downstairs. I knew it must be Dr Leonardo and I whispered to her that when the doctor arrives they start hurting people, doing bad things to them. Soon after that they came to get her. It was then that she quickly put a finger in her mouth and started chewing vigorously. A few seconds later she began to writhe, she fell on her side, moaning, her face looked horrible, and soon she was dead. She looked dead and it turned out that she was dead.'

'Do you know what had happened?'

'They said she'd swallowed poison, that she had poison in her mouth, ready to swallow. That night Dr Fleury went mad, he shouted at everyone. A real commotion. Then he ordered them to take her down to the yard.'

'To the yard. Always this yard. What was there?' The therapist is growing impatient.

'There was a drum. One of those big metal drums. There was this garage, right at the back of the yard, it seemed more like a tool shed. They took the prisoners there, and a few hours later they brought out some large canvas sacks, tied up tightly. They loaded them into a pick-up parked by the front gate, ready to leave, and soon they left. I think they took these sacks a long way because it always took a whole day before the pick-up returned. Then they washed everything out in the yard with a hosepipe, they scrubbed the whole place and sprinkled it with bleach. They put clothes and other things into the drum and burned them. Two or three times they called me to help them wash the cement floor around the drum. It was always the same two men who did the work out there. Two men from the military police in Minas Gerais. They were always called this, "the military policemen from Minas". They were never called by their names.'

'Do you know what they did with the prisoners in that garage?'

Jesuína doesn't seem to hear. The therapist repeats the question more forcefully.

'What did they do to the prisoners down there, Jesuína?'

Jesuína puts her head in her hands as if she's trying to stop the question reaching her ears. She stays like this for a while, then pulls her chair close to the therapist and whispers, as if she's telling a secret:

'Once I was alone in the house for almost a whole morning. The military policemen from Minas had left early in the pick-up, saying that they'd run out of canvas sacks, that the shop where they bought them was a long way away, that they wouldn't be back for quite a while. Dr Fleury had already left for São Paulo in the early hours of the morning. I was alone, in charge. I went down to the back yard to see for myself. The garage didn't have a window. The door was locked with a chain and padlock. A wooden door. But I could peer in through the hole they'd made in the door for the hosepipe. I saw some butcher's hooks, just like the ones you see in any butcher's shop, and a big table and butcher's knives, saws, hammers. That's what gives me nightmares. In them I see bits of bodies. Arms. Legs, all cut up. Blood, a lot of blood.'

Jesuína gives a deep moan and starts to cry. Soon her crying takes her over completely, and she begins to convulse, slowly slipping from her chair. The therapist catches her before she hits the floor, pulls her up and hugs her. They both stand there, crying.

Giving up literature

Ever since he'd carefully climbed the stairs of the archdiocesan office, step by step, for his meeting with the archbishop, K had thought of writing down his observations. Not only had they been very strong that day, but the meeting had also had a special symbolism for him, because an authority in the Catholic Church, the same church that had once nurtured Torquemada,[1] was welcoming him warmly and becoming deeply and sincerely involved in his search for his daughter, something that not even the rabbis had been prepared to do.

But days went by, weeks, months, and he didn't write anything. He regretted this now, wishing he'd at least kept a diary of his contacts, his searches. Now that he'd lost hope, and all he had to fill his days was the agony of not having anyone else to search for and talk to, the only thing left was his old profession as a writer.

He decided to write his masterpiece. It was the only way of making a clean break with everything he'd written before, of redeeming himself for having paid so much attention to Yiddish literature that he had not picked up the signs that

1 Tomás de Torquemada was the Inquisitor General for the Kingdoms of Aragon and Castile in Spain, who carried out the extermination of converted Jews, being responsible for about 1,200 *autos da fé* in which the 'heretics' were burnt at the stake.

his daughter was getting involved in clandestine political activities, some of them so blatant they were clearly disguised cries for help that he in his oblivious state hadn't noticed.

He began where he'd always begun: jotting down observations, one by one as they arose, on bits of cardboard that he made out of empty shirt boxes; at a second stage, he'd bring some of these jottings together and then begin his narrative, always writing in Yiddish and always writing by hand. Only later would he type up his text on the special typewriter with Yiddish characters that he'd brought back from New York. This was how he wrote all his articles for newspapers and magazines.

Because Yiddish is written with Hebrew letters but has a Germanic syntax, the enemies of Yiddish, including Ben Gurion[2] himself, had called it a monstrous language, a linguistic Frankenstein. But K had always rejected these criticisms, saying that they were the monsters, those in Israel who had turned their back on such an expressive language, used by so many great writers.

K went as far as filling up several scraps of cardboard with his impressions of episodes, conversations, events around his daughter's disappearance. But when he tried to turn these notes into a coherent narrative, something didn't work. He wasn't able to express the feelings that had often overwhelmed him, in the meeting with the Archbishop for instance.

It was as if the essential element was missing. It was as if the words, though chosen with great care, hid or mutilated his feelings, instead of expressing the fullness of what he'd experienced. He found that he couldn't express his tragedy in the limited meaning of a word, in the excessively precise constraint of a concept, in the vulgarity of an idiomatic

2 David Ben Gurion, leader of the working-class party Mapai, led the process for the creation of Israel and was its prime minister for fifteen years.

expression. He, who'd won awards for his Yiddish poetry, was unable to find the words to transcend linguistic limitations.

Could it be a limitation of the Yiddish language? Was it possible that the Jewish people, who'd been through so much, were unable to express suffering in their own language? That couldn't be the case. Although it was only in the last hundred years that Yiddish literature had been created as such, the language itself was over a thousand years old and was spoken by more than ten million people.

Besides this, K reflected, since Yiddish was a language of affectionate diminutives, a domestic language spoken by craftsmen and very poor people, by cart-drivers and street sellers, it was self-evident that feelings could be expressed in Yiddish. You only had to look at the tales of Sholem Aleichem and Bashevis Singer.

But he couldn't manage it. Was it because Yiddish was too chaste a language to express the obscenity that had happened to him? Swear words disgusted him, like all of his generation who were educated in a heder. This linguistic fastidiousness never left them, not even those like him, who rejected religion.

Gradually K realised he was facing a different barrier. Of course, words always limit what you say, but that wasn't his main problem: his block was moral, not linguistic. He was wrong to want to turn his daughter's tragedy into the subject of a literary work. Nothing could be more wrong. To be proud of writing something beautiful about such an ugly thing. Worse still, because this wretched Yiddish had been the reason why he had not seen what was happening under his nose – the tricks his daughter had used to stop him visiting her, the sudden journeys to unknown destinations.

He recalled a day when she, in a hurry – perhaps frightened – had disturbed his Saturday meeting with writers and he'd ticked her off, without even looking her properly in the face, without trying to find out what she wanted. Just think of it, to try to make literature out something like this. Impossible.

That night K tore up his notes, cut them into tiny pieces, and put them into the rubbish bin. He swore he would never again write in Yiddish. He almost admitted that Ben Gurion had been right when he'd claimed that Yiddish was the language of the weak, of those who let themselves be killed without reacting, as if they already expected to be punished for their sins, whether they had committed them or not.

He was also pushed into this decision by a chance event: he wanted to tell his granddaughters in Israel about everything that had happened. And his granddaughters didn't speak Yiddish, only Hebrew. That night K wrote his first letter to a granddaughter in Israel in impeccable Hebrew, just as he'd learnt it as a child in the heder. He was no longer a renowned writer making literature out of the wrongs that had befallen his daughter: he was a grandfather recording a family tragedy for his grandchildren.

The Army almanac

'This one would sell his own mother.'
The man is emphatic and precise, as one would expect from a four-star general. His language is coarse, because that's how you were supposed to speak in the barracks. Trained as a leader, he speaks in clipped, rough sentences, even though he doesn't give orders any more. He was stripped of his command and cashiered from the army for opposing the military coup in 1964.

His hair may be white but he is still vigorous and forceful. As he goes through the list of men he commanded and his colleagues, he is precise and objective in his descriptions, as if he's classifying a collection of spiders. On a table in front of him the Army Almanac lies open, with the names of all the officers, from lieutenant upwards, of the three branches of the army: infantry, cavalry, and artillery.

His younger brother, a famous surgeon, operated on and perhaps saved the lives of many businessmen and bankers who were involved in that cursed coup. But even this wasn't enough for the general to keep his rank. The injustice of his expulsion has heightened his critical perception, and further loosened his tongue; it is clear that, despite being a military man, he is an honourable person.

'This one here, as well as selling his mother, would dance on her grave.'
The Almanac looks like a telephone directory. Abbreviations after each name indicate the steps in each officer's career since he entered the Military Academy; they register every change in rank, every course he took in the Cadet School, and all additional training he has received since then. Divided into three parts, one for each of the branches, the book is a mirror of military life.

'This one here was top of the class.'
Someone who comes first in his class in the Military Academy will always be referred to as 'top of the class'. What a good thing, you might think. Surely it shows that our Army is so principled that knowledge and even intelligence are the criteria for advancement? Perhaps also hard work? So it's an Army that prioritises intellectual excellence?

Well. It's not quite like that.

'Only those in the artillery had to study.'
They are the ones who have to learn trigonometry and ballistics, to work out the angles of fire, to know how to compensate for the wind direction, the calibre and weight of the payload, and to calculate the enemy's movements. They deal with complex equations. They learn how to think things through rationally. That's why they've become the brains of the Army; they're the only ones with a strategic vision. They organised and directed the military coup.

'The rest of them are a gang of boneheads; the cavalry are the worst of all.'
As it is an army that hasn't fought a war for thirty-five years, there are no medals for bravery on the field; there are no dangerous missions, no extreme situations that test units or

individuals. Instead, what counts are classroom marks, the precision of the military salute, the elegance of the uniform, the sheen of the boots, the knowledge of war scenarios that will never be put into practice, and their imaginary logistics. All on paper, theoretical. Drawers and drawers of maps and plans for strategic attacks, tactical advances and retreats.

'The main hypothesis was a war with Argentina, but that was something that was never going to happen, just a way of keeping them busy.'
There is a meticulous scheme for recording each promotion in this dull military life. In an officer's progress through the command structure or in administration, all due procedures are respected. But, as happens in every bureaucratic organisation, the rules only serve to legitimise an inherent favouritism, never to install a proper meritocracy. Decisions are taken on the basis of friendship. What matter are bonds of loyalty. Not real loyalty, because that is unconditional. But calculated loyalty, required for survival in the internal war for bureaucratic promotion.

'The greatest bottleneck occurs in the progression from colonel to brigadier-general. Only one in fifty colonels will become a general. Those who don't make it are thrown out.'
In this world of office meetings, the casualties don't happen on the battlefield but in the short-lists for promotion submitted by the general staff to the high command, which has the final say. Officers can't remain stuck in the same rank. Those who aren't promoted fall without a shot being fired.

'In order to be promoted to general, a colonel needs to belong to a network with a general who can look after his interests.'
Long before he becomes a colonel, the officer has made sure

he belongs to a group. He sucks up to a general, flattering him and grovelling before him.

'This one here was my student in the parachute course. He became a stickler for legality, like me. When I opposed the coup, he followed my example. He was kicked out when I was. But most of my underlings betrayed me and joined the coup-makers.'

There are two ways of getting promotion: currying favour with a general or blackening the name of the other candidates on the list. Sucking up and betraying. These tactics can be alternated or used together. On occasion, a candidate has even been known to betray the general who's supporting him. Treason is the other side of the coin from opportunistic loyalty. In this bureaucratic military organisation, an officer never confides in two people at the same time. Always just one; then, if he's betrayed, he'll know who betrayed him. Treason is also an art.

'Prestes[1] adopted this tactic in his column and then incorporated it into the security norms of the Communist Party, where it was even more necessary because the party was almost always banned. He finished up making the party even more secretive than it had been before, with never more than two people meeting together, and even then speaking in whispers.'

Habits create values. The practice of treason and dissembling became incorporated into the military ethos. Values were turned upside down. Everyone became an Esterhazy,[2] with no Dreyfus. Instead of bravery, cowardice. No honour, only

---

1   Luis Carlos Prestes was an army officer who in the mid-1920s was one of the leaders of an insurrectionary movement that led the so-called Coluna Prestes, the Prestes' column, on a 25,000-km march through the Brazilian countryside. After the rebellion failed, Prestes embraced communism in the 1930s and became the leader of the Brazilian Communist Party.
2   Charles Esterhazy was a French officer who spied for Germany, with all the blame for the spying activity being falsely ascribed to a Jewish officer, Alfred Dreyfus.

dishonour. The poor became the enemy. Wickedness was taken to an extreme. Take the beheadings in Canudos;[3] the killing of prisoners in the Araguaia, some of them minors; the chopping up of bodies in 1974 to 'disappear' people. In the wake of this addiction to brutality came a paradoxical crime that goes against the grain of a bureaucratic organisation, although it follows the logic of the new values: the suppression of all evidence.

'This is the only general, as far as I know, who ordered a stop to the torture.'

Although he was extremely right-wing, this general was a spiritualist.[4] When he found out about the torture, he paid a surprise visit to Barão de Mesquita and ordered them to put an end to it at once. Spiritualists are not allowed to maltreat any creature, human or beast, because they believe in reincarnation; for them bodies are the temporary homes of the souls of our ancestors and as such they must be venerated. You might be torturing your great grandmother, or even your mother if she's already deceased.

'But as soon as he left, it all started up again. And he didn't sack anyone or even make a complaint, publicly or internally.'

According to the military doctrine of the time, called adverse psychological warfare, the enemy could be anywhere, or it might not even have declared itself an enemy yet; actors, naive youngsters, rebellious girls, progressive priests: all were possible enemies. According to this doctrine, only torture would reveal a suspect's subversive propensities. It was just like during the

---

3 Canudos was a settlement in a very poor area in the north-east of Brazil which was set up by a messianic leader who was calling for a return to monarchy. It successfully stood up to three army expeditions, but a fourth one in 1897 led to its complete annihilation. All of its inhabitants were killed, many of them by decapitation.

4 Spiritualism is a mainstream religion in Brazil.

inquisition, when torture was supposed to make the demons come out of the bodies of the witches and expose the deceits of the heretics and forced converts.

'This one here is the cleverest and the cruellest of them all. He's from the artillery, of course. He knew that the game was up, so he proposed a gradual, controlled, and safe relaxation of the dictatorship. He's part of the old guard and could have enlisted in Brazil's expeditionary force to fight in the Second World War, but he didn't. To this day no one knows why: did he support the Nazis? Did the Americans veto him for supporting the Nazis?'
The ex-general closes the almanac. We'll finish here. That's enough for you to get the picture.

The extortionists

Yes, it was him. Although he'd seen him only once and in the dark, K recognised his features, his sweaty oval face, his bushy moustache and broad forehead. He's a sergeant. He'd introduced himself that night as a general, but he's only a sergeant. He still remembered how they'd pushed him into the back seat of the car, the bogus general on one side and a skinny man with an evil look about him on the other.

Why hasn't the skinny man been charged too?

The bogus general said he had found his daughter. He would bring him a letter from her in exchange for money. But it had all been a charade. And now the imposter was being put on trial – not by him, as he wasn't interested in revenge; he only wanted to find out what had happened. It was the military themselves who had brought charges against him.

Before then, K had never heard of the Tribunal of Military Justice. When he received the summons, written on official paper and signed by a general, he felt excited. At last, the military authorities were summoning him to deal officially with the disappearance of his daughter.

According to the nameplate in front of him, a colonel is presiding over the session. On one side of him is another colonel, and on the other a civilian wearing judge's robes.

Next to the judges' high dais, on the same level as the small, empty courtroom, sits the accused.

At times K believes it was bound to happen. He'd known that at some point an opportunist would appear, offering information in exchange for money. Perhaps someone would even say he could save his daughter if he were paid a very large sum. Hadn't something like this happened in Poland, when the members of his party had pooled resources to get him out of prison?

But in Poland it had been different. Although the repression had been harsh, they had registered the arrests, informed the family, allowed prison visits. And then there had been a court case, with a prosecution and a defence. There people hadn't disappeared.

He thought of the police and military as ordinary people, some good and some bad. Some might even help because they have feelings; others are extortionists and, even among these, some do what they promise and others simply suck all they can get out of the victim. These, you might say, are sick people, like this imposter sergeant. But he'd had to seize any chance, and he'd had little opportunity to know who he was dealing with. He'd done what he'd had to do.

At other times he felt he'd been a fool to believe that money could break down the wall of silence surrounding the disappearances, for that was something that people far more important than him had tried to do and failed. He was not to know that forty years later this wall would still be standing, unbreached. But even back then he knew that everything had been carefully organised so that no one would be able to find out anything. How could I have been so naive? he asked himself at these moments.

The testimonies begin. He tells them exactly how it happened. The only thing he leaves out is that the one who told him about the bogus general was a trainee lawyer. Even though the youngster had behaved badly. At the crucial moment, he'd not turned up, and left him on his own on that dark corner of Barão de Limeira Avenue, at the mercy of the extortionists whom he had recommended.

How could K alone have worked out what to do? It's true he'd been mistrustful. He'd asked the men for a note, signed by his daughter using the affectionate nickname that only he used, as proof that she really was alive. The criminals had no way of knowing what the word was and they had got it wrong.

What K doesn't understand is why after this he still went to the meeting. At times, he thinks he only went because he wanted a fight. But together with this was the faint hope that they really had found his daughter and couldn't bring the note signed by her because of some unexpected problem. Yes, that was what he must have felt on that dark corner. A glimmer of hope. It was that hope that had betrayed him.

The story appeared in the newspapers. This wasn't K's initiative, because he felt ashamed of being hoodwinked. He'd talked about it at the meeting of the families of the disappeared to warn them, so that none of them would fall into the same trap. A journalist had found out and published the story. The bogus general was on trial not because he'd extorted money, but because the armed forces had emerged badly from the incident. This was quite clear to K.

The testimonies continue. Now they interrogate the sergeant. He stutters out an apology. He admits that he's never seen the girl in prison, that he's invented everything, from start to finish. He doesn't mention his accomplice, the thin guy.

K isn't interested in what happens to the imposter. That's all over. It's ended. He's come to ask about his daughter in this one and only contact with the justice system. Her disappearance was after all what it was all about. It was for this reason that he'd begged the young lawyer to come with him to the military tribunal. He'd know how, at the proper moment, to ask for an investigation into his daughter's disappearance. But the trainee lawyer had failed him again. He hadn't turned up.

K recalls once more how, in the silence that had followed his request to a top lawyer that he apply for habeas corpus for his daughter, this trainee had interrupted and hurriedly mentioned the possibility of a contact with 'people inside the system'. Here it was a question of money, he said, lowering his voice, and had nothing to do with the habeas corpus; it was a parallel process.

K should have realised that the coolness with which the top lawyer received this suggestion was a warning: be careful, this young man's wet behind the ears, he has good intentions but he doesn't know how things work. That was where his mistake started. Not understanding what the top lawyer meant. He was a responsible, committed person; you could see it in the fearless way he defended all those persecuted for their political beliefs, as if humanity itself were at stake.

But how could he have turned down the trainee's suggestion after the top lawyer had told him, with great regret, that a request for habeas corpus would be turned down, because the military had banned habeas corpus in cases of political imprisonment? We're living a paradox, he remembers the top lawyer saying: they admit they have political motives for making arrests, but they don't admit they have made political arrests.

K is now listening without interest as the military prosecutor puts his case. He thinks about what the extortion has meant for him. His main concern is not the money he's lost; after all, what's thirty thousand cruzeiros compared with his daughter's life? The price of a car compared with something utterly priceless. Nor the embarrassment of people knowing that he'd been taken in, nor his awareness that he'd weakened at the decisive moment, when he already knew it was a charade.

No, the worst had come later, when another opportunity arose, when that rabbi suggested that he should contact a man with a German name, who lived in Rio and had already saved a girl. A Jewish girl. He knew the girl's family and he'd been to check it out. It wasn't a lie: the girl was living abroad. The only known case.

K arranged a meeting by phone and went to Rio on the night bus. The man, about 40 years old, elegantly dressed in a linen suit, didn't even ask him to come in. On the pavement in Copacabana Avenue, he said that the police chief who was in charge of everything owed him a big favour. That once he'd transported a stiff in his boot for the policeman. A corpse, he repeated, when he realised K didn't understand what he meant. He'd got the police chief out of a right mess. He could find out if his daughter was still alive. But it was going to cost him a great deal of money. Do you own your home? If so, sell it. It's going to cost you the price of a house.

K didn't believe him. He didn't take up his offer. Perhaps because so much time had gone by. Or perhaps because he'd already been tricked once and wasn't going to be tricked again. That was the main impact of the extortion. If that first charade hadn't happened, perhaps he would have gone ahead with the German. He would have taken the risk.

It's very likely that it wouldn't have got him anywhere, that his daughter was already dead by then, as everyone is saying. But K wouldn't be suffering the agony of thinking he hadn't done everything he could to save her. And the person to blame for that was this bastard sitting in front of him. But K doesn't hate him. Rather, it's disgust: contempt for those who take advantage of other people's woes and give them more pain.

The presiding judge bangs the table with a little wooden gavel and reads out the sentence. The accused, Sergeant Valério, is to be stripped of his rank and sentenced to a year's imprisonment, after which he will be dismissed for damaging the reputation of the Armed Forces by spreading the false information that civilians were detained in military installations for criminal purposes.

'But my daughter?' asks K, getting to his feet on an impulse after the sentence is read. 'Where is my daughter?' he shouts.

The presiding judge looks at him threateningly. He bangs the table again and declares the session at an end. He adds in a loud voice: 'The records show that no civilian is held in military installations. As the convicted prisoners' confession demonstrates, it was all a charade.'

'But my daughter?' K stutters, looking around the empty courtroom.

The three judges get up abruptly all together. Two enormous soldiers, wearing military police helmets and armbands, take the accused out through a side door. Another two, just as tall and strong, come up to K and show him the exit. One on one side and one on the other, they push him and force him to leave.

The Council meeting

Around a long, heavy mahogany table with carved edges, just as a University table should have, sit eight prestigious professors from the Institute of Chemistry, some heads of department and some famous scientists (including Ivo Jordan, a specialist in uranium isotope separation; Newton Bernardes, an expert in materials physics; and Metry Bacila, a pioneer in marine biology). Giuseppe Cilento, who helped bring together departments and researchers scattered in different parts of the University of São Paulo to form the Institute, was also present.

The Institute of Chemistry is renowned for its scientific rigour, which it owes to the influence of the two Germans who founded it, Heinrich Hauptmann and Heinrich Rheinboldt, both of whom fled to Brazil to escape Nazism. At the time of this meeting, it was only five years old. Built with money from the Ford Foundation, the Chemical Complex, as it is generally called, occupies the whole of the eastern hill of the campus.

This is the forty-sixth monthly meeting of the Chemistry Council, the Institute's governing body. The date is 23 October 1975. It is nineteen months since the disappearance of K's daughter, who is described in the university staff list as a postgraduate assistant lecturer. On the agenda is case

174899/74 from the University Council, requesting that her contract be rescinded for 'dereliction of duty', according to clause IV of article 254 in the regulations governing staff behaviour. Another item on the agenda is the proposal to re-employ the retired lecturer Henrique Tastaldi, who also happens to be on the three-member commission that is calling for the lecturer to be dismissed.

The account that follows is imagined, on the basis of the minutes of the meeting. Many years later the Vice-Chancellor's office publicly recognised that an injustice had been committed, but it never admonished any of those involved, or contacted the family to apologise. None of those present at the meeting ever expressed regret for what they had done.

Presiding at the meeting was the Director of the Institute, Professor Ernesto Giesbrecht, the patriarch of Brazilian chemistry, a member of the Brazilian Academy of Science, holder of the National Order of Scientific Merit and a disciple of Rheinboldt himself, who had supervised his doctorate. Giesbrecht has died since the meeting. We don't know what was going through his mind. We can only guess:

This is going to be a painful meeting. I hope it ends quickly. After all, we received an ultimatum. If Heinrich was alive, he wouldn't believe that this could be happening. After all, he fled from Germany because of his wife's Jewish family. But I'm sure he would be doing the same as me. After all, he founded the Chemistry department and wouldn't like to see it destroyed because of a single person, and moreover an ordinary lecturer who has no more than a doctorate. If she'd been a head of department, had a post-doc, but she's just an assistant lecturer ... What matters in the chemistry department is the leadership, we've got to look after the people at the top. Thank goodness the voting is secret, so no one is going to be exposed, no one will know who voted for the dismissal. I hope there are no problems.

According to the minutes, what he actually said at the meeting was:

> I have great satisfaction in welcoming for the first time as a member of the Chemistry Council Professor Otto Richard Gottlieb, recently appointed full professor in the Department of Basic Chemistry. It is an honour for this Council to be able to count on his collaboration. As the minutes of the forty-fourth meeting have been unanimously approved, we shall move onto the first item on the agenda, which is the offer of a new contract to retired lecturer Henrique Tastaldi.

Lecturer Francisco Jerônimo Sales Lara, from the Philosophy Faculty, wonders if he should say something. We can imagine the thoughts running through his head:

> *This Tastaldi is a scoundrel. Now he's going to get both a lecturer's salary and a pension. It's a done deal. They approve taking him on again and, in return, he backs the sacking of the lecturer. It's his reward for being complicit in repression. This wouldn't have happened in the Philosophy Faculty. Everyone knows she was taken by the secret service. Her father was here, there were adverts in the newspaper, reports, she's on the archbishop's list of twenty-two disappeared people. My God, where is this all going to end? What a bunch of reactionaries and cowards these people are. And they say that most of them are Jews fleeing from Nazism or have these Jews as their supervisors.*

Now Sales Lara speaks. He measures each word. His contribution is recorded in the minutes:

> Undoubtedly Professor Tastaldi is a historic figure who made a great contribution to the development of biochemistry. As well as this, he has personal qualities that make him a much loved figure. However, I don't think that it is opportune for the Chemistry Institute to hire him. I am against offering new contracts to retired lecturers, and I think this can only be justified when it is absolutely impossible to find

another person. This is not the case here. There are many high-level people with doctorates and post-doctorates, both inside the country and abroad, who would be interested in the terms we can offer. It is our obligation to offer these people university career opportunities.

The renowned Professor Metry Bacila speaks. According to the minutes:

I cannot fail to register my admiration for the great contribution Professor Tastaldi has made to the University of S. Paulo to which he has dedicated all his life in research, teaching and doctoral supervision. We must also remember the enthusiasm with which Professor Tastaldi devoted himself to university reform, contributing with all the wisdom he has acquired as an eminent professor, along with his collegiate spirit not often encountered even within the university ... [It] will be proud to boast that it still has him as a member of its teaching body.

Professor Giuseppe Cilento speaks. The minutes register:

I must also express my gratitude for the courteous help I received from Professor Tastaldi during all the time I was head of department.

Then Professor José Ferreira Fernandes speaks:

A few days ago we were all sorry to see Professor Tastaldi retire, but the Institute has a policy of not giving new contracts to retired professors.

When the proposal from the biochemistry department was put to the vote (with secret voting), the result, checked by lecturers Gilberto Rubens Biancalana and Yukio Miyata, was twelve votes in favour and three against. So the proposal was approved by two-thirds of the members of the Chemistry Council.

Giesbrecht continues:

We now come to the next item on the agenda, the proposal to end the lecturer's contract. Let me explain to the meeting that the lecturer has not worked since 23 April 1974. Her absence was reported to the relevant body in the Vice-Chancellor's office which, when consulted as to what action should be taken in accordance with the current legislation, ordered that an investigation be undertaken, with a view to dismissing her. Professors Henrique Tastaldi and Geraldo Vicentini, along with Dr Cássio Raposo do Amaral, a member of the Judicial Consultancy, made up the commission that carried out the investigation, and it has proposed that the lecturer be dismissed for dereliction of duty. There will now be a vote on this matter, in accordance with the current legislation.

Giesbrecht shifts around in his chair, as if he's uncomfortable. Let us continue to imagine what he might have been thinking at this stage of the meeting.

What a disagreeable meeting this is proving to be. It's true I never liked the young woman and she wasn't a brilliant student, but she took her job seriously and worked hard. Her research into molybdenum for her doctorate wasn't easy but she made a good job of it. What option do we have? They say that the call from the Vice-Chancellor's office was unequivocal. You have until the end of the week to follow the regulations and sack her. In fact, the ultimatum came later than we expected. I know they say she was disappeared, it was even reported in the press. But there's no proof. The government denies it. Of course, it's obvious that, whatever really happened, they would deny it. But God knows what she was involved in. The regulations are clear, and don't leave us any room for manoeuvre. And if I don't dismiss her, as Director of the Institute I might be accused of prevarication. That is, if I'm not accused of something worse, like connivance with subversion or something of the sort. It's my duty as a scientist to preserve the institution. Not to give them any excuse to invade the campus or to expel staff. After all, the young woman had no right to endanger an important institution like ours.

At the far end of the table, the other founder of the

department and the oldest of them all, Professor Gottlieb, tries to guess what is going through the mind of his colleague and academic rival. Gottlieb is Jewish and left Czechoslovakia at the time of the German occupation. In Brazil he set up various research laboratories into natural products. He might well have been thinking along these lines:

I know the Director received an ultimatum from the legal department: sack the lecturer before the end of the week. I rather liked this young woman. A hard worker. And much more interested in culture than the others. One day I found her reading The Magic Mountain. The way she looked — she always seemed a bit sad — made me think of my cousin Esther, who never got used to being in exile. A bastard, this Giesbrecht, ein schlechter Charakter, and they say he was a disciple of Heinrich. He should have slammed down the phone on whoever called him. Instead of letting the legal department have their way, he should have taken advantage of the university's prestige to force the government to provide some information, to get it to say what she was charged with. But they're doing the opposite, sacking her as if she'd simply failed to turn up to take her lessons, and not responding to a kidnap. In other words, they are covering up the kidnap. Scham. How shameful. The problem is that he's the boss and it's very difficult to know how to oppose him.

The representative of the assistant lecturers, Gilberto Rubens Biancalana, had arrived late for the meeting and now thinks about speaking, but decides not to, perhaps because he's frightened. He must have been thinking something like this:

My colleagues were scared when I suggested we should hold a meeting to decide on the position to take. Now I've got to decide how to vote on my own. I'm not going to jeopardise my career for a lecturer I don't even know well and has been up to God knows what. If Giesbrecht and Gottlieb had come up with an idea, to postpone the decision or something else, I might have backed them, but to act alone.... Or if this Newton Bernardes, who's come from Physics, had done something. He's already a full professor, holds important positions ... he has a name, prestige.

Miriam, who represents the teaching assistants, doesn't say anything. She thinks well of the lecturer, who worked hard and was kind, but she's afraid:

It's so sad what's happened. Terrible. I don't know why all these important people haven't done anything about it all this time. That was the mistake they made. If they'd made a big fuss as soon as she disappeared, perhaps everything would have been different. If it had been the Institute putting pressure on the Vice-Chancellor's office, demanding that it got rid of those shits from DOI-Codi[1] who've installed themselves there, not given the legal department time to exert pressure. All this talk about 'due process', 'evidence', it's all rubbish, something they've got from Falcão.[2] And me here, without the support of anyone, having to take part in this charade. I ought not to have come, invented an excuse and stayed away. Why don't they all stand up and say no? It's shameful, to let a person be kidnapped and then accuse her of not turning up for work.

Professor Luiz Roberto Pitombo doesn't say anything. Perhaps he was analysing the situation along these lines:

I don't know what this young woman was involved in. She never wanted to talk about what she was doing and I didn't want to ask her. I suspect it was something serious. Useless leftism, lack of

---

1   DOI-Codi was Brazil's most savage agency of repression during the dictatorship.
2   Armando Falcão was justice minister at the time.

strategic vision. Even so, of course we ought to express our solidarity and denounce the repression. The problem is the situation in this council, in this institute. There's no point in getting myself into trouble for an individual case. We have to have a broader horizon in this struggle, strategic values. It's a real shame and wrong. But in the present correlation of forces, one vote against, an isolated voice, isn't going to do any good and might well harm our cause.

Professor Giesbrecht explained that the commission had taken its decision on the basis of evidence, as stated in their report, and had attached great importance to the declaration by Minister Armando Falcão that there was no record of the lecturer being arrested.

The secret vote on the report calling for the dismissal of the lecturer then took place. The report was approved by thirteen votes, with two spoilt votes, and the decision was reported to the Chancellor of the University, Orlando Marques de Paiva. Two days later, on the authority of the State Governor, Paulo Egydio Martins, the lecturer's dismissal was recorded in the official gazette. He is another one who has never apologised.

Streets and names

The building site was in the back of beyond, a long way from the city centre, with plots cheap enough for people to be able to build their own houses. It was here, thanks to a law passed by the municipal council on the initiative of a left-wing councillor, that each of the streets had been given the name of a disappeared person, forty-seven streets for forty-seven disappeared people.

Even before the streets had been properly marked out, the councillor himself had driven stakes into the ground at the main crossroads and nailed on to them blue plaques with the names of the disappeared people. Just their names, without the date of their birth and, obviously, without the date of their death.

Family members, no more than fifteen, most of them from São Paulo, met in front of the Glória Hotel in Rio and travelled by minibus across the Rio–Niterói bridge. It was a long journey. Although exhausted, tired of everything, even of life, K had decided to take part in the homage to his daughter and son-in-law.

Once there, they held a short ceremony. The councillor made a speech, praising those who had fought against the dictatorship, and announcing the beginning of a new era with different values. Naming the streets after the disappeared, he said, was a way of making sure future generations would know of the importance of democracy and human rights. It was a good speech, thought K; both the speech and the street names were trying to give meaning to so many lost lives.

An elderly white-haired lady spoke on behalf of the families. K couldn't remember her name, but he recognised her from that first meeting in the archdiocesan office when she'd given an account of her son's disappearance that was both warm-hearted and embittered. She spoke well on this occasion too. Again, she was both warm-hearted and embittered. They were all moved.

After they had been given a site plan, they separated into small groups, each looking for the street bearing the name of their disappeared loved one. It took K some time to find his streets, one named after his daughter and the other after his son-in-law. When he found them, he asked one of the others to take photographs, as he still didn't know how to use a camera.

By the time they left it was getting dark. As they drove away, K saw the only large sign for the new building site, a green billboard with big red letters saying: Vila Redentora. K feels outraged, although it is a coincidence; 'redentora' – redemption – is the name the military have given to the coup. K tries to control his anger. What's important, he tells himself, is the homage paid to the disappeared. It takes time, but he calms down.

As the minibus took them back, he began to pay attention to the names of the roads. Strange that he'd never done so before. When he had first arrived in Brazil, he'd been curious about everything. But later he'd stopped noticing things. Until all this business with his daughter. He saw one of the street names – Fernão Dias Street. Where he lived in São Paulo there was a street with the same name. They'd told him once that he'd been a famous hunter of Indians and runaway slaves. Then, to his dismay, he spotted a street with the name General Milton Tavares de Souza.

He knew who he was: he would never forget this name. The chemist's son had spoken about him. Dom Paulo the Archbishop too. He was the man who created the DOI-Codi, and it was there that they'd taken Herzog and killed him.[1] He was these bastards' Lavrentiy Beria, the Brazilian Himmler,[2] who had said that no holds were barred if they were killing subversives. And now he'd had an avenue named after him, an important avenue. How could they have done such a thing? Name it after a scoundrel, 'a menuveldike roitsech', he swore in Yiddish.

Indignant, K now scrutinised the street names and was scandalised to see the name Costa e Silva on the Rio–Niterói Bridge. Unbelievable, a majestic creation like that, almost nine kilometres long, carrying the name of the general who had decreed the fearful AI-5.[3] In Poland they named avenues after kings and marshals. There were many called Pilsudsky and Marzalkowska,[4] but he had united Poland, he was a hero, not a villain. Imagine if in Germany they'd named a street after Goebbels or in the United States after Al Capone, or if in Lithuania they'd paid homage to the hangman Muravyov.[5]

The problem arises, K thinks, when someone is a hero for some and a scoundrel for others, like Bogdan Khmelnytsky,[6]

1   CODI-DOI was one of cruellest of the military dictatorship's agencies of repression; here in October 1975 a well-known journalist, Vladimir Herzog, was killed under torture.
2   Lavrentiy Beria was the head of the Soviet secret police during its most ferocious period. Heinrich Himmler was head of the Nazi secret police.
3   Institution Act no. 5, was the decree issued by the military in 1968 closing down Congress and annulling individual rights, such as the right to habeas corpus.
4   Marzalkowska is a derivation of 'Marshal', and so an implicit tribute to Pilsudski.
5   Mikhail Muravyov-Vilensky (1796–1866), a Russian military officer who repressed the Polish-Lithuanian rebellion in 1863, and had hundreds of people hanged.
6   Bogdan Khmelnytsky (1595–1657) led the revolt of the Ukrainian Cossacks against Polish domination, massacring Jews in the process.

who ordered the pogroms in Ukraine and was regarded as a hero there, perhaps for that very reason. He even has a city named after him. K feels incensed. He's still fuming when they reach the centre of Rio with its impressive Getúlio Vargas Avenue. This man was a civilian. K had felt some sympathy for him – the 'father of the poor' of his early years in Brazil. But he was a dictator and his head of police, Filinto Müller, had been bloodthirsty. He'd killed and tortured a lot of people. It would be the last straw if a street had been named after Müller. But I expect there is one somewhere, K thought.

How is it that he'd never noticed this strange Brazilian habit of honouring gangsters and torturers and coup-makers as if they were heroes or saviours of the world? He'd written so much about life in Brazil but he'd never spotted this. In other countries they were righting these wrongs. In Warsaw they'd changed the name of the traditional Gesia Street to Anielewicz.[7] It's true that a rotunda still bore the name of that fascist and traitor Roman Dmowski,[8] but he felt sure the name would be changed soon. He'd read in a newspaper that the French were going to remove the name Pétain from their streets after they'd discovered that during the occupation he'd given the go-ahead for the deportation of sixty-five thousand French Jews, including six thousand children, to Drancy, from where they were taken to concentration camps and exterminated.

On the bus back to São Paulo, he was calmer; the country's main motorway was called Via Dutra, and, as far as he knew, Dutra had been a democratic President, although he'd also been a general and anti-Semitic. He'd expelled communists from Congress and made it difficult for Jews fleeing the war

---

7   Mordechai Anielewicz was the leader of the uprising in the Warsaw Ghetto.
8   Roman Dmowski was the leading right-wing politician in Poland in the inter-war years. He was a Social Darwinist and anti-Semitic.

to settle in Brazil, although he welcomed the volksdeutsche.[9] But, as far as K knew, he hadn't killed or disappeared anyone.

As the bus approached São Paulo, it went under a bridge bearing the name General Milton Tavares Viaduct. That criminal again. K had been under that bridge many times but he'd never noticed the name. Hundreds of people must go under it every day, he thinks, and young people and children seeing the name will imagine he's a hero. Now he understands why the streets named after the disappeared are in the back of beyond.

9 The volksdeutsche were German-speaking ethnic minorities who lived in eastern Europe.

Survivors, an afterthought

Although each life story is unique, all survivors suffer to some degree from melancholy. That's why they don't talk to their children and grandchildren about what's happened: they don't want them to be affected by this malady before they've even started to build their own lives. They don't talk to their friends about it either, and if their friends bring the subject up, they feel uncomfortable. K never told his children about the death of his two sisters in Poland, just as his wife tried to avoid talking to them about the loss of her whole family in the Holocaust.

Survivors can only live in the present for a while. Once they've got over the shock of having survived, once they've managed to resume normal life, the demons of the past re-emerge with unimaginable vigour. Why did I survive and not them? It's common for survivors to be racked by this feeling of guilt much later on, decades after they suffered their loss.

In the film *Sophie's Choice*, a Polish woman is forced by a Nazi guard to choose which of her two children she wants to survive: the boy or the girl. If she'd been Jewish, there wouldn't have been a choice, as both of them would have been sent to the crematorium; but, since she is Polish, the guard invents a new game: the mother has to choose and, if she refuses to do so, they will both be killed. 'Sophie's choice' became an aphorism, meaning an impossible choice, in which either option is equally painful.

But why did the German soldier force the mother into making this impossible choice when it would have been simpler for him either to kill the children and the mother, or to make the choice himself? Sadism? Perhaps. But sadism with a purpose, because in this way the criminal transfers the guilt for the child's death to the mother. Wasn't she the one who made the choice? Over the years, this feeling of guilt takes possession of Sophie's soul until, when she is very old, a survivor from the war living in the United States, she commits suicide, unable to bear any longer the guilt that she should never have had to feel.

Guilt. Always guilt. The guilt of not having noticed the fear in a certain look. Of having behaved one way instead of another. Of not having done more. The guilt of being the only one to have inherited the parents' meagre inheritance, of owning books that once belonged to another. Of having received a paltry compensation payment from the government, without even asking for it. Behind it all, the guilt of having survived.

Milan Kundera says that Kafka's inspiration was not totalitarian regimes – although this is the usual interpretation – but family life, the fear of being criticised by his father. In *The Trial*, Joseph K meticulously examines his past life, looking for the hidden error, the reason why he is being tried. In the short story 'The Judgement', the father accuses his son of being selfish and condemns him to 'death by drowning'. The son accepts the bogus blame and throws himself into the river as docilely as later Joseph K will hang himself, believing that he too made a mistake, just as the system claimed. Just like Sophie.

In the same way, survivors are always revisiting their past, searching for that moment when they might have prevented the tragedy but for some reason failed to do so. Milan Kundera invented the term 'family totalitarianism' to describe the set of mechanisms for creating feelings of guilt that Kafka uncovered. We could call our version 'institutional totalitarianism'.

That is because it is obvious that full information about the kidnappings and executions, about when and how each crime was committed, would do away with all the grey areas that lead us to believe that, if only we'd behaved differently, we could have prevented the tragedy.

That was why, although paltry, the compensation offered to the families of the disappeared was paid out quickly, without the families demanding it – in fact, in order to pre-empt such a demand. It was a way of burying the cases without burying the dead, without creating the space for an investigation. A subtle manoeuvre that turns each family into an involuntary accomplice of a certain way of dealing with the past.

'Institutional totalitarianism' ensures that the guilt, fed by doubts and impenetrable secrets and reinforced by the compensation, remains within the survivors as a personal and family trauma, and does not become the collective tragedy that it was and continues to be half a century later.

The meeting at the barracks

'What's the point of dying a thousand times a day? Die once and end
your agony in peace.'
H. N. Bialik[1]

K has known the barracks for more than fifty years. In all that
time he's never imagined that one day he'll be going there to
take cigarettes to political prisoners. When he first arrived in
Brazil, it was just a small garrison built by the Public Force,
as the police forces were then called, to look after the pastures
where the Force bred its chestnut-coloured horses. Almost
every day K would travel in his salesman's horse-and-cart along
a track that reached the fields on the far side of the garrison.
He'd known some of the men stationed there, as well as the
commander, Lieutenant Júlio.

In those early days, there weren't department stores as
there are today and you could only get a bus into the centre of
São Paulo along Cantareira Avenue, the one asphalted road.
Women welcomed the travelling salesman's visits, with his
supply of pretty fabrics, blouses, nightdresses and other goods,
all of which could be paid for in instalments. K was fascinated
by his customers; the back yards with their *jabuticaba* trees;[2]
the Portuguese women with their fields of cabbages, the

1   Hayim Nahman Bialik was one of the pioneers of modern Hebrew poetry and is widely
recognized as Israel's national poet. These lines are an English version of the translation into
Portuguese by J. Guinsburg of one of his poems.
2   The *jabuticaba* is a native tree from the tropical forest that has grape-like fruit that grows
directly on the trunk and branches.

mulatto women. He'd never seen a mulatto woman in Poland. He listened to their stories, and wasn't bothered if they didn't buy anything.

He came back weighed down with the cabbages and bananas he'd been given. As soon as he'd unharnessed the mare, he'd go round to see his elder brother, who lived next door, and tell him about that day's adventures, the people he'd met, their stories. Then he'd write articles about what he'd seen, publishing them in Yiddish newspapers in São Paulo, Buenos Aires and even New York. He'd become well known among the Jews in Bom Retiro and it was through them that K found someone to put up the capital for his shop. K's role in the partnership was to bring in the customers.

By then, there were more asphalted roads and it was the customers who made the journey to his shop. They compared K as he was before his daughter disappeared with K now, and they pitied him. Before, K wanted to listen to their stories. Now they had to listen to his lamentations. One of them, Sergeant Ademir, whose family had been one of his first customers, told him about the arrival of political prisoners in Barro Branco. There were almost 30 of them, he said. Perhaps one of them would know what had happened? The commander, Coronel Aristides, was his brother-in-law and Ademir could see if he'd let the old man visit the prisoners and talk to them.

The commander agreed, although strictly speaking he shouldn't have, as K wasn't related to any of the prisoners. And so there K stood, under a hot sun one Saturday, anxiously holding a pack of cigarettes and bars of chocolate. Big buildings that he didn't recognise occupied part of the old pasture. That one's the military police hospital, explained Sergeant Ademir, who was accompanying him, pointing to a large, two-storey building.

The prison was further on, almost the last building. It was the military police's own prison, explained the sergeant, where they locked up policemen who'd committed crimes. One semi-isolated wing was used for political prisoners.

As he made his way slowly towards this wing, K went back in his mind to his time in prison in Poland. He remembered again how they'd dragged him in chains through the streets of Wloclawek to humiliate him in front of the tradesmen. Not so different from what he felt now, he observed, as he dragged his battered body across the square, though there were no chains this time. He felt very tired. It was fourteen months since the disappearance of his daughter.

In Brazil he'd joined the same left-wing Zionist party he'd helped to found in Poland – the cause of both his imprisonments – but this time he devoted himself almost exclusively to cultural activities, mainly the promotion of the Yiddish language. Everything he'd done in the last fifty years was worthless self-deception – that's how he saw it now. His books, his novels, his stories, his fascination for this back-of-beyond country that had eventually swallowed up his daughter.

He felt that the premature loss of his daughter was a punishment for the way he'd been constantly absorbed in literature, in his writer friends. That's where he'd put his energy. His elder son had turned his back on him long ago. He'd left the country in a rage and had never made peace with his father. K hadn't known how to handle his youthful rebellion, his bad behaviour at school. His other son had been the well-behaved one, but he'd been introspective, taciturn, and had also left the country.

K had lavished his affection on his daughter. Everything he hadn't given to his two sons or to his wife, who'd been ill with cancer, he made up for in his feelings for her. But he realises now that this devotion to his daughter was also a trap that destiny had laid for him, part of the tragedy: first making him feel so much for her, and then taking her away from him.

K clutches the bag with the cigarettes and the chocolate

tightly. They are getting close to the political prisoners' wing. The sun is bothering him. He is sweating profusely on his forehead, on the whole of his face. He gets a handkerchief out of his pocket with his left hand and wipes his face. Then he recalls the hot Polish spring when his mother took Passover food to him in prison. They were ten siblings, living on the edge of starvation, but his indefatigable mother always managed to bring him a bread roll or a cooked egg, or some special food on feast days.

It was during those days in a Polish prison that he'd discovered the importance of cigarettes and chocolate. This is why he had them with him now. What he carried in his bag was his identity, his memories, the balance-sheet of his life. A life cycle drawing to a close, with the end joining up with the beginning. And in the middle, nothing. Fifty years of nothing. K felt very tired. His legs were giving way beneath him, he was feeling faint. As they reached the political wing, the sergeant was supporting him.

The prisoners were waiting for him: all men, and most of them young. They were well dressed and clean-shaven. But K could tell from their looks that they'd been in prison for a long while. He knew that look, that unmistakeable look. It was the look he'd had 50 years ago.

The sergeant explained that, thanks to a hunger strike, the prisoners had won an improvement in their conditions. They could now leave their cells, they had a collective kitchen, they were able to organise a huge number of courses. Many of them were teachers. After these explanations, the sergeant left.

They arranged chairs in a circle. K sat in the front. He put his bag on the floor and began to tell them the story he'd told so many times. But it was as if he was telling it for the first time. He looked intently at one prisoner and then at another. He stumbled over his words. In the middle he started speaking in Yiddish. Like a refrain he repeated the words mein tiere techetel – my beloved little daughter. He was speaking with the heavy Polish accent of his first days in Brazil.

The prisoners listened to him in silence, their eyes fixed on K's sweating face, as if hypnotised by the sunken sockets of his red and rheumy eyes. The old man's suffering made a deep impression. Many of them would never forget that moment. One of them, Pedro Tierra, recalled decades later 'the worn-out body of a very old man, sustained by two eyes – two flames – that were the very incarnation of despair'. Some of them had known his daughter and son-in-law; they'd been members of the same underground organisation; they all knew the story, even the names of those who'd given them away. They knew they'd both been dead for a long time.

Suddenly, K began to sob. The prisoners remained silent. Some of them had tears in their eyes. K leant forward and put his hands over his face. He couldn't contain his sobs. He felt very tired. Then he bent down and tried to pick up the cigarettes and the chocolate bars so he could hand them out. Perhaps he was trying to stop himself crying.

At that moment, he collapsed.

Alarmed, the prisoners in the front ran to help him. Without letting go of the pack of cigarettes, which he was now clutching tightly in his left hand, K lay down on the

floor, breathing heavily. Three of the prisoners lifted him up slowly, holding him under his back and his legs. They carried him as if on a stretcher to the nearest cell and placed him on a bunk bed.

K remained with his eyes shut for almost ten minutes, breathing deeply, his chest heaving. Then he opened his eyes and saw the political prisoners gathered around him; high up on the wall at the back of the cell, the familiar little barred window with its promise of sun and freedom. He felt at peace. Very tired, but at peace. He handed over the pack of cigarettes. Then his hands relaxed and his eyes closed.

Message to comrade Klemente

Klemente,

I don't know if I should still call you comrade after what you said to the Paris group about the Organisation not existing any more. Perhaps your declaration was a trick to mislead the repression, but we also know that you've been in contact with the communist party.[1]

Well, you ought to know that the repression doesn't accept that the Organisation has died. They're still hunting us down. In the last week five comrades from different organisations – including our Yuri – were captured and disappeared. Nowadays all those taken prisoner completely disappear. Already this year forty-three have disappeared, apart from the ones we don't know about.

We ought to have rethought things long ago. Didn't the Old Man[2] always say that it isn't enough to know who your enemy is, you also need to know what your objectives are? Since the kidnapping of Elbrich,[3] we've only had losses but no reappraisal,

---

1 The Brazilian Communist Party (Partido Comunista Brasileiro) was opposed to the armed struggle.
2 A reference to Joaquim Câmara Ferreira, killed in 1970, the successor to Carlos Marighella in the leadership of the ALN, one of the main groups in the armed struggle against the military dictatorship.
3 Charles Burke Elbrich, US ambassador to Brazil, was kidnapped by armed organisations and freed after the freeing of political prisoners.

with no clear definition of our objectives. Dozens of young comrades have fallen. At the same time, instead of greater rigour in our security, we've slipped into a sense of invincibility, we're not taking the same care as before, arranging meetings by phone, completely absurd.

We've suspected for some time that the dictatorship doesn't want to take prisoners any more. We should have analysed this, carried out self-criticism, recognised that we're isolated. Perhaps, if we had done so, we could have saved a lot of lives. But instead we decided to fight on to the end, even if it got us nowhere. That's where the madness began. This religious thing, this 'if I had ten lives, I'd give ten lives'. What we're doing, in fact, is playing into the hands of the dictatorship, which wants to wipe us all out. It seems to me that some comrades have become morbidly fatalistic, believing that there's no alternative but to die like Che.

Márcio warned against the useless sacrifice of so many people. He said we were heading towards collective suicide. Do you remember? It's because of him that I'm sending you this message. He argued that it made no sense to wage war without the support of any social class and without political actions. And after the Old Man was taken, he challenged those who thought the Organisation was in a position to prepare a counter-offensive.

In his heart, the Old Man was already aware of what was happening. So much so that he let some comrades go, those he thought had a chance of living another life. He was aware of the hopelessness of it, and he didn't want these deaths on his conscience. At the same time, as you can see from the way in which he died, he was also preparing for his own death.

Another error was not to distinguish between old and young comrades. A commander who has fought for fifty years has been through victories and defeats, has had children and grandchildren – that's one thing. Someone aged only 20 hasn't lived yet, doesn't know anything – that's something quite different. It wasn't by chance that the Old Man called himself old. But he made a huge mistake. After the death of Mariga,[4] he should have let everyone go, immediately. There were neither the objective nor the subjective conditions to justify a retreat to the countryside. Someone should have given the order to stop it all. And that someone was the Old Man. That was the right moment.

What astounds me most today is the way we've gradually lost the notion of totality, the capacity to see the whole. And, as we don't see the whole, we don't see the relations between the parts, the contradictions, the limitations. We've become blind, totally alienated from reality, obsessed by the armed struggle.

You know, although Mariga was the great leader, the one who set the line, it was the Old Man who articulated everything; he didn't take part in the tactical groups but he held everything together. After he fell, it made no sense to continue. That's what we instructed Márcio to tell the leadership. Their response was to reject our proposal, without any argument, without any new policy guidelines. They acted completely irresponsibly.

When, after the death of Mariga, the Old Man went to Cuba to talk to comrades there, it was already clear that the time for armed struggle was over. There was talk about rebuilding political action, going to factories, abandoning the Cuban model of revolution, which wasn't working for Brazil. Zaratini, along with many others, put this to the national leadership in a document. The Dissidents, as they were called, were also in favour of demobilisation, disappearing off the map, vanishing in the face of such brutal repression. Aluysio also told them in Paris that we had to stop. Many people said so. But the Old Man wouldn't listen. He invented this strategy of tactical urban offensives to keep the flame alive, while at the same time preparing rural bases for a long-term strategic struggle. Always the same pretty words – tactics and strategy, but without any basis in reality.

And he was the one who began to talk about treason. To

---

4   A reference to Carlos Marighella, the founder of the ALN, who was killed in 1969.

suggest that there was an informer in our midst. In fact, as we now know, there was more than one. But the idea took off, not because there was any evidence, any concrete facts, but because of the succession of defeats. It became an obsession, a substitute for a hard look at reality. It became a way of putting pressure on those who were beginning to hesitate. Instead of being dealt with as a question of security, treason became an ideological issue. Worse than that, a moral issue, as if to leave the struggle was the same as betraying it.

You played the chief role in the meeting which decided that Márcio should be executed on suspicion of being a traitor. The latest people to fall prove what we suspected all along: Márcio wasn't the informer. He was executed because he'd asked the national leadership to allow him to give up the clandestine struggle. The Organisation lied in its communiqué: Márcio wasn't executed to protect the Organisation. He was executed to send a message: anyone who thinks about leaving will be dealt with as a traitor. He hadn't committed any crime. He hadn't informed on anyone. They sentenced him to death because of his wish to leave. This was so obviously the case that Milton argued against it.

Instead of allowing Márcio to leave, as he'd requested, you took the opposite view and in this way made it impossible for the Organisation to put an end to a struggle we'd already lost. We could have saved many lives. It was what we needed to do. Not least because Tavares, who betrayed the Old Man, wasn't the only informer. There's at least one other person today going to the old meeting places, trying to identify us.

Even under the capitalist system of justice, a person isn't sentenced to death unless the verdict is unanimous. Yet you passed a death sentence without evidence, without specifying the crime. You've adopted the ways of the dictatorship, even its police language. In its communiqué, the Organisation calls Márcio an 'element'. Then you executed Jaime, even after he'd told you everything he'd said to the police under torture. There the message was that whoever speaks, even under torture, is a traitor. As if it's possible to judge someone who's been tortured. You created a taboo around the issue. You incorporated the dictatorship's methods of terror. Then it was Jacques' turn. Jacques had also spoken under torture, and had also gone to the leadership to warn them. Three executions. When you killed Jacques in June 1973, it was already two years since we'd suffered the heavy losses that had decimated the Organisation.

And now you go to Paris and say that our Organisation doesn't exist any more. That's very easy to say. Of course it doesn't exist any more. It hasn't existed for three years. But what do we do with our documents? Are we to burn them all? How do we get rid of all traces of our existence? How can we stop them killing us, even if we put an end to all our activities? The repression is so determined to do away with us all that we need the Organisation to organise how to end the Organisation. We don't know how to get out of this trap.

This is the last message you will receive from me. It's possible that, by the time you receive it, my partner and I will already be dead. We feel that the circle is closing around us. Don't try to find out how this message got to you and don't keep it. The best thing you can do after reading it is to destroy it. I've given a copy to the few comrades who are still alive, asking them to do the same.

Rodriguez

Postscript

Three decades and a bit have gone by. Suddenly, two months ago, a telephone call to this same house of mine, to this son of mine who never knew his kidnapped and assassinated aunt. A woman introduces herself, first name and surname, saying she lives in Florianópolis. She's just back from Canada, she tells him, where she went to visit relatives, and they were talking in Portuguese in a restaurant when a woman came up to them, saying she was Brazilian and giving her full name, the name of the disappeared aunt. The woman left her number for us to contact her.

I didn't phone back. I remembered those early months after her disappearance. Whenever we got close to a sensitive part of the system, false information appeared about where she was to tire us out and demoralise us. This call, I concluded, is a reaction to the TV programme that the Brazilian Bar Association (OAB) put out a few months ago, in which an actress played the role of a disappeared woman. The call from the supposed Brazilian tourist came from the repressive system, which is not yet dismantled.

São Paulo, 31 December 2010

To the reader

Everything in this book is invented but almost everything happened. I let recollections flow directly from my memory just as they came, after being buried for years, without confirming them through research, without completing them or shaping them with records from the time. There are references to documents in just two stories and then only as a recourse in the narrative.

Then, adopting story-telling techniques, I put these memories in imaginary situations. I brought together incidents that had happened at different times. Other incidents I made up almost entirely. I invented solutions to fill gaps that came from what I'd forgotten or from what my subconscious had blocked.

Each fragment emerged as a complete, separate story. They appeared not in chronological order, but arbitrarily, as buried memories came to the surface. Often they took on unexpected shapes. This again forced me to treat the incidents as literature, not as history.

The book's unity comes from K. This is why the fragment that introduces him comes straight after the opening. And the fragment that puts an end to his suffering is almost the last in the book. The order of the other fragments is arbitrary.

Bernardo Kucinski

Bernardo Kucinski, a Brazilian journalist and university teacher, is the author of several books published in Brazil and abroad, including *The Debt Squads – the US, the Banks and Latin America* (Zed Books, 1988) and *Politics Transformed: Lula and the Workers' Party in Brazil* (Latin America Bureau, 2003).

Enio Squeff, a Brazilian journalist and art critic, has published five books. He began painting and drawing twenty years ago. His work has been exhibited in Brazil, Cuba and Colombia. He has illustrated, among other works, Homer's *Odyssey*, Kafka's *Metamorphosis* and Hemingway's *The Old Man and the Sea*.